ROBOT REVOLUTION

JAMES PATTERSON is the internationally bestselling author of the highly praised Middle School books, *Homeroom Diaries*, *Kenny Wright: Superhero*, *Jacky Ha-Ha*, *Word of Mouse*, *Pottymouth and Stoopid*, and the I Funny, Treasure Hunters, House of Robots, Confessions, Maximum Ride, Witch & Wizard and Daniel X series. James Patterson has been the most borrowed author in UK libraries for the past ten years in a row and his books have sold more than 350 million copies worldwide, making him one of the biggest-selling authors of all time. He lives in Florida.

Also by James Patterson

MIDDLE SCHOOL BOOKS
The Worst Years of My Life (*with Chris Tebbetts*)
Get Me Out of Here! (*with Chris Tebbetts*)
My Brother Is a Big, Fat Liar (*with Lisa Papademetriou*)
How I Survived Bullies, Broccoli, and Snake Hill (*with Chris Tebbetts*)
Ultimate Showdown (*with Julia Bergen*)
Save Rafe! (*with Chris Tebbetts*)
Just My Rotten Luck (*with Chris Tebbetts*)
Dog's Best Friend (*with Chris Tebbetts*)
Escape to Australia (*with Martin Chatterton*)

I FUNNY SERIES
I Funny (*with Chris Grabenstein*)
I Even Funnier (*with Chris Grabenstein*)
I Totally Funniest (*with Chris Grabenstein*)
I Funny TV (*with Chris Grabenstein*)
School of Laughs (*with Chris Grabenstein*)

TREASURE HUNTERS SERIES
Treasure Hunters (*with Chris Grabenstein*)
Danger Down the Nile (*with Chris Grabenstein*)
Secret of the Forbidden City (*with Chris Grabenstein*)
Peril at the Top of the World (*with Chris Grabenstein*)

HOUSE OF ROBOTS SERIES
House of Robots (*with Chris Grabenstein*)
Robots Go Wild! (*with Chris Grabenstein*)

OTHER ILLUSTRATED NOVELS
Kenny Wright: Superhero (*with Chris Grabenstein*)
Homeroom Diaries (*with Lisa Papademetriou*)
Jacky Ha-Ha (*with Chris Grabenstein*)
Word of Mouse (*with Chris Grabenstein*)
Pottymouth and Stoopid (*with Chris Grabenstein*)
Laugh Out Loud (*with Chris Grabenstein*)

DANIEL X SERIES
The Dangerous Days of Daniel X (*with Michael Ledwidge*)
Watch the Skies (*with Ned Rust*)
Demons and Druids (*with Adam Sadler*)
Game Over (*with Ned Rust*)
Armageddon (*with Chris Grabenstein*)
Lights Out (*with Chris Grabenstein*)

For more information about James Patterson's novels, visit
www.jamespatterson.co.uk

Or become a fan on Facebook

HOUSE OF ROBOTS

ROBOT REVOLUTION

JAMES PATTERSON
AND CHRIS GRABENSTEIN

ILLUSTRATED BY JULIANA NEUFELD

CHAPTER 1

You'd think a house full of robots would run like a well-oiled machine.

You'd be wrong.

I mean it *used* to run that way. But lately? Everything seems a little out of whack.

Take, for instance, the Groomatron 4000.

It's a high-tech, fully automated robot that's programmed to dry my hair in ten seconds flat. But today, instead of blowing hot air, the Groomatron nearly sucked all the hair off my head! I almost had to go to school bald.

Maybe the Groomatron thinks it's a vacuum cleaner, too.

I need to talk to Mom about that. I'm Sammy Hayes-Rodriguez, and all of the bots in my house were designed and engineered by my mother, Dr. Elizabeth Hayes. She's kind of the absentminded professor/genius type. I'm sure it'll take her all of ten seconds to debug the hair dryer, once she gets around to it.

Meanwhile, at 7:25 a.m., it's off to my sister Maddie's room for breakfast and a quick game of Spine Spinner Trivia, another invention of Mom's that makes it easy to exercise our minds and bodies at the same time.

The Breakfastinator whips up today's special: blueberry pancakes with sausage patties, melted butter, and hot maple syrup.

We wolf down our food and really don't pay too much attention to the fact that our blueberries taste like raisins and the melted butter tastes like burnt cheese and the maple syrup smells like onions. Guess the Breakfastinator is on the fritz, too. Doesn't matter. We're too excited about playing Spine Spinner Trivia, where, if you get an answer wrong, you have to twist your body like a pretzel on a mat decorated with flashing pads of colored light.

Since the mat's a robot (named Matt, of course), it asks the questions, too.

"Maddie, which city is nicknamed the Windy City?" barks Matt's robotic voice, which Mom modeled on my gym teacher, Coach Stringer.

"Chicago!" answers Maddie.

"Correct. Sammy? According to the rhyme, who picked a peck of pickled peppers?"

"Peter Piper!"

"Sorry. The correct answer is Peter Pan."

"Um, no it's not," says Maddie.

"Yes it is," insists the robo-mat. "Left hand to red square, Sammy."

"But…"

"Drop and give me ten!"

"Ten dollars?"

"Ten push-ups!"

All righty-o. Need to talk to Mom about the glitch in Matt's operating system, too. But not right now, because it's time to head to school.

"C'mon, Sammy!" hollers Dad from downstairs. "C'mon, E. You guys will miss the bus!"

Who's E? My bro-bot. And if he's late for school, Maddie will be, too!

CHAPTER 2

Meet E, short for Egghead.

Mom named him that because he's super intelligent.

He's also my little sister Maddie's eyes, ears, and nose at school. If they're serving beef burritos in the cafeteria, E will let her know how awesome they smell.

"Sorry," I say when I bound down the stairs

SAY HI TO MY BRO-🔲🔲T!

to the kitchen. "I was sort of tied up in Maddie's room."

"We don't want to be tardy, Samuel," says E, who still sounds a little robot-y when he talks. (Don't worry. We're working on it.)

"¡El tiempo no espera a nadie!" adds my dad. His name is Noah Rodriguez. His family came to America from Mexico. Living with my dad is like living with my own Spanish tutor.

"Time waits for no man," I translate.

"¡Sí! ¡Perfecto!"

"El tiempo también espera a ningún robot," adds E, who, with his newly installed system updates, now understands and speaks Spanish, French, Mandarin, Farsi, and Third-Grade Girl (because Maddie's in the third grade, so E has to know what to squeal at and what to giggle about). "We must make haste, fly like the wind, and shake our tail feathers."

E also has a very extensive built-in vocabulary generator.

Why does Maddie need E to go to school for her?

Well, my sister has something called SCID. That doesn't mean she has a South Carolina ID, like a driver's license or something. SCID is short for *severe combined immunodeficiency*. Basically, it means Maddie's body has a hard time fighting off any kind of germs. If somebody coughs near her, she'll wind up with a major infection.

Maddie may only be eight, but she's already spent a couple of *years* in hospitals.

That's why she has to stay home, inside her sterile bedroom, while E goes to school for her.

Yep, Maddie can never leave the house. Actually, she hardly ever leaves her room. For an eight-year-old who loves to do *everything,* that's really tough.

"It's no biggie," is what Maddie always says when anybody asks her about her condition. But if it were me, if I had to be a boy in a bubble, trust me: it'd be bigger than a biggie. It'd be a *huge*-ie.

"Cross-referencing my internal GPS monitor and available real-time performance data from the South Bend, Indiana, public school system," reports E, "we should immediately arrange for an alternate mode of transportation to Creekside Elementary."

In other words, we missed the bus. (Like I said, I still need to work with E. Get him to stop using twenty words when four will do.)

"No problem," says Dad. "I'll drive you guys to school this morning in our brand-new electric SUV!"

"Cool," I say.

And it really is, because my mother just invented the most awesome, unbelievably amazing, technologically slick ride in the world! It's like a huge smartphone with wheels.

Trust me: this is going to blow you away.

CHAPTER 3

Our new car is so new, it's experimental.

Instead of "new car smell," it has the aroma of adventure, research, and exploration, all of which sort of smell like a toaster plug after it short-circuits.

After Mom's robots won a major mechatronic football game at the University of Notre Dame, where she's a professor, my parents sold our *other* new car because they said it was a dinosaur (even though it only had two thousand miles on it).

I guess compared to the electric SUV-EX, any set of wheels would have to be called a dinosaur. Or a clunker. One of those.

"Hey, Sammy! You missed the bus!"

Meet my second best friend since forever, Harry Hunter Hudson, or, as I sometimes call him, Triple H, or just Trip. He would be my number one best friend, but Maddie already has that title.

Since he's here telling me something I already know (which is something he does a lot), this is probably a good time to tell you a little about Trip. And remember, no matter what I say, he's still my best friend who isn't related to me.

Trip is kind of a klutz. Maybe even a goofball. He constantly says the wrong thing to the wrong people at the wrong time. He tells knock-knock jokes at school—during the morning moment of silence. His clothes (including his socks) never match, his backpack makes him look like he's part Tyrannosaurus rex, and every day for lunch he eats the exact same smelly thing: peanut-butter-and-banana sandwiches.

He's not exactly popular at school. In fact, he doesn't have too many friends except me.

Then again, I don't have too many friends except him.

And E. Thank goodness we have E.

"Hello, Trip," says my dad. "Did you miss the bus, too?"

"Well, I was at the bus stop when the bus pulled up but I noticed that Sammy wasn't there so I decided to come over here, so yeah, I think I missed it, unless, you know, it's still at the corner waiting for me to come back, but I kind of doubt it even though—" Trip's eyes widen as he admires the electric SUV-EX. "Can the car make more Pop-Tarts?"

"Yeah," I say. "I think so."

"Awesome!"

"You are welcome to ride to school with us," chirps E. "Unless, of course, you have some objection, Mr. Rodriguez."

"Of course not," says Dad. "The more the merrier. Liz designed this vehicle to seat six. And get this: according to her, one day soon, not a single one of us will have to sit behind the steering wheel! The car will drive itself!"

"Indeed," says E. "It will be a fully autonomous, automatic automobile."

"Will it pick its own radio stations, too?" asks Trip.

"No way," I say. "If it did, we'd have to listen to that stuff Mom likes. Mozart."

"Because Mozart was a genius!" the car exclaims.

Oh, did I forget to mention that the electric SUV-EX also talks?

CHAPTER 4

When we sit down in our seats, the SUV-EX remembers who we are—by our weight, not by anything gross, like how our butts smell. Then it adjusts our seat belts accordingly.

"Good morning, Noah, Egghead, Samuel, and Harry Hunter Hudson. Welcome aboard!"

"Wow," says Trip. "It remembered my butt from that time we all went out to get ice cream."

"Excuse me, Harry Hunter Hudson," the car says in a jolly voice that reminds me of my aunt Jennifer, "but golly, you could choose a better word than *butt*. How about *posterior, derriere,* or *gluteus maximus?*"

"I agree," adds E. "There's no need to be crude, Trip. Remember, a *rump roast* sounds much better at the butcher shop than a *butt roast*."

"Okay," says Trip. "Thanks, you guys!"

Yep, our new car does a whole lot more than just give GPS directions. Yesterday, it taught me how to play badminton.

We're about to pull out of the driveway, so I glance up at Maddie's bedroom window.

Just like always, she's there, waving good-bye to us.

McFetch, our robotic and hypoallergenic dog, is up there with her, wagging his tail.

This may sound weird, but even though Maddie's my little sister and, you know, shorter than me, I always look up to her. Even though she's stuck in her room, she never lets it get her down.

"Hang on, guys," says Dad. "We're running late. It's blastoff time!"

He stomps on the gas pedal, but since this car is electric, it doesn't really use gas. So I guess it's just "the pedal."

We cruise up the block without making much noise—well, once the car stops giving Dad driving tips.

In fact, the electric SUV is almost completely silent except for its random bird chirps. Mom added those as a safety feature so people could hear us coming.

"Oh, Mr. Rodriguez," says Trip, "I finished those pages you let me read. Your new book is going to be awesome!"

"It's better than awesome!" I say. "It's going to be a comic masterpiece."

"Yes," says E. "It will be a veritable *Don Quixote* of graphic novels!"

"Who's Don Quixote?" asks Trip. "A friend of yours, Mr. Rodriguez?"

"Don Quixote," says the dashboard, sounding like the smartest girl in class, "is a Spanish novel by Miguel de Cervantes Saavedra. It was originally published in two volumes: one in 1605, the other in 1615."

"Thank you, Soovee," says Dad.

Soovee is what he calls the electric SUV-EX, usually when he wants it to stop blabbing at him.

"I'm glad you guys like my new book," he says. "I'm almost finished with it."

"Well, please hurry, sir," says Trip. "I can't wait to see what happens next to the Ninja Manatees on Mars."

In case you didn't know, my father, Noah Rodriguez, is also the world-famous Japanese manga artist Sasha Nee, the guy who created the super-cool series Hot and Sour Ninja Robots. Dad's created a bunch of other graphic novels, too. Some hits. Some misses.

Dad glances up into the rearview mirror to look at Trip and me in the backseat.

"So how are things going on your science project, boys?"

Uh-oh.

Trip and I exchange glances.

The science project.

Talk about mistakes.

CHAPTER 5

Trip and I are working together on an amazing idea for the upcoming science fair at Creekside Elementary.

If we can pull it off, we'll be famous. Superstars of science. No, super*heroes* of science. Like Iron Man!

Then again, it might just turn into a total train wreck, which is what it's sort of been ever since we started working on it. Fortunately, before I have to say, *"Well, Dad, our science project happens to be a complete and total disaster,"* the SUV starts blabbing again.

"I'm sure Sammy will," says E. "However, I can predict, with ninety-nine percent certainty, that Trip will be eating a peanut-butter-and-banana sandwich."

"Actually," says Trip, "today I'm going with banana and peanut butter."

"I will make a note for future car rides," says Soovee. "Oh Samuel? You'll be pleased to hear that the Fighting Irish of the University of Notre Dame are a two-point favorite in their football game this Saturday."

"Excellent!"

"And Mr. Rodriguez?"

"Yes?"

"You need to pick up a gallon of milk, some challah bread, a dozen eggs, and a bottle of vanilla extract if you still plan on making French toast for everybody this weekend."

"Right. Thanks."

"You also need new shoelaces."

"Got it."

"And now, our joke for the day."

"That's okay, Soovee," says Dad. "We're almost at school."

"This will only take a second."

"No, seriously," says Dad. "We don't really want to hear—"

"Why did the scarecrow get a raise? Because it was outstanding in its—"

And then, before it can say "field," the car completely dies.

It stops chattering, stops monitoring our seat cushions, stops moving forward, stops giving driving advice to Dad. It basically stops doing all the really cool stuff it's supposed to do.

It's just dead.

Right in the middle of the drop-off lane at school.

CHAPTER 6

Dad jiggles the keys in the ignition. "Come on, Soovee."

Behind us, all sorts of cars start honking. School buses, too. Trip and I sink down in our seats. This is extremely embarrassing.

Lena Elizabeth Cahill, the cutest girl in the fifth grade, is on crossing guard duty. She stomps over to our stalled vehicle, gestures with her flag for Dad to roll down his window, and then props her hands on her hips so she can glare at us.

"You cannot park in the middle of the driveway, Mr. Rodriguez," she says.

"I know. I'm not parking. I'm having, uh, technical difficulties."

Story of my life.

"Well, sir, because of your 'technical difficulties,' I'm having a traffic jam during morning drop-off!" says Lena, her reflective neon sash glinting in the sun. "This is not acceptable, Mr. Rodriguez. Not on my watch."

"Perhaps I can suggest a solution," says E, leaning forward so Lena can see him.

"Oh, hi, E," giggles Lena, completely changing her tone. "I didn't see you there."

I think Lena Elizabeth Cahill has a crush on E. I also think she doesn't know I exist.

"This is a very experimental vehicle," E explains. "One day, perhaps soon, it will be able to drive and park itself."

"That's fantastic," says Lena. "You think you could make it, like, do that today?"

"No. However, my arms are outfitted with, if I do say so myself, an array of impressive hydraulics. I am able to lift extremely heavy objects quite easily. I suggest that all passengers disembark, and I will tow the car over to the curb."

"Wow," says Lena. "You're as strong as a tow truck?"

"Not to brag, but yes. I am. The automobile club tried to recruit me for roadside assistance, but I told them I was too busy matriculating for Maddie Hayes-Rodriguez."

We all climb out of the vehicle.

"What does 'matriculating' mean?" Trip mumbles as we shuffle over to the sidewalk.

"Going to school," I say. E likes to use the big *m* word a lot.

"Oh," says Trip. "Then why didn't he just say 'going to school'?"

"I know, I know. I'm working on it." Getting Mom's school-stand-in robot to sound more like a real kid is supposed to be my responsibility.

E marches around to the front of the SUV and hooks one finger under the front bumper. Then, with a *WHIR*, a *CLICK*, and a big *FERUUUUUUMPPPHHH*, he hoists the front end off the ground and drags the whole car over to the curb.

Show-off.

Everyone applauds. Dad steps aside to call some-body on his cell phone. Probably a real tow truck.

E takes a slight bow.

"Thank you," he says to the assembled crowd. "On behalf of Dr. Elizabeth Hayes and myself, we regret any inconvenience our ongoing quest for scientific knowledge may have caused you this morning."

"Actually," a kid I've never met before pipes up, "your so-called quest for knowledge is idiotic, foolish, and laughable."

All righty-o.

Something tells me this new kid and I aren't going to be besties.

CHAPTER 7

"**D**o I know you?" I say to the new kid.

"Don't be absurd," he replies with a haughty huff. "How could you possibly know me when we've never even met? This is my first day matriculating here at Creekside Elementary."

Trip tugs on my sleeve. "That guy said 'matriculating,'" he whispers. "Just like E."

"I know," I say out of the corner of my mouth as we walk through the school's front doors. "I heard him."

"Be careful, Sammy," warns Trip. "Little Mr. Know-It-All could be a ninja robot disguised in strange clothes."

Now that Trip mentions it, the new kid does look a little goofy. Nobody else at Creekside comes to school in a navy-blue blazer with gold buttons, pleated khaki pants, a white shirt, and a striped tie. I mean, this is elementary school, not church.

"Allow me to elucidate as to why your electric SUV is a ludicrous idea."

"Huh?" I say.

E comes over to translate. "He wants to explain

his negative reaction to Mom's new car."

The kid sniggers. "I didn't realize that robotic devices such as you had mothers."

"If I might be permitted a slight play on words," says E with a grin, "Dr. Elizabeth Hayes, my creator, is the *mother* of many inventions."

Trip laughs, so I do, too.

"And she's the one who designed that abomination?" The kid flaps his hand toward our dead SUV.

"Sammy?" asks Trip. "Is he calling your new car a Sasquatch?"

"No," says E. "However, by using the word *abomination,* he is suggesting that the electric SUV-EX is a disgrace, a mistake, and an error."

Funny. Error is what I used to call E before I got to know him better.

"Wait a second," I say. "Who the heck are you, anyway?"

The boy taps the breast pocket of his blazer. I see three *R*s embroidered there in gold thread. The thread matches the buttons.

"I am Randolph R. Reich. Fifth grader. I'm never wrong, because I'm always Reich."

Since he pronounces his name "Rike," his dumb joke makes E chuckle.

"Very amusing," says E. "However, Randy—"

"Randolph."

"Sorry. My bad. However, Randolph, we all make mistakes—such as my gaffe just now using the more familiar form of your first name."

Randolph shakes his head. "Not me, Mr. Roboto. I never make miscalculations. Your 'mother,' on the other hand, made a colossal blunder when she decided to engineer a battery-powered SUV."

"Oh, really?" I say, because I don't like anybody, especially new kids who've never met her, trash-talking my mom. "How come?"

Randolph sighs. "It's so obvious. Do I really need to explain my reasoning?"

I shoot him a look that lets him know he'd better.

"Fine. An SUV, or sport-utility vehicle, is primarily intended to be used for rugged, off-roading purposes."

"We go camping," I say defensively. "Well, we did. Once."

(With Maddie's SCID condition, the great outdoors isn't all that great.)

"And where, pray tell, would you recharge your battery-powered vehicle when you went on a camping excursion? Where, for that matter, would you even find an electrical outlet in the wild? Would you, perhaps, plug it into the nearest pine tree?"

Okay. Randolph R. Reich might not be very nice, but he's actually correct.

I hate when that happens.

He's also attracted an audience. And once again, they're all laughing. At E, me, and, even though she's not here, my mom.

"Plug it into a pine tree!"

"Ha!"

"Sammy and his whole family are such weirdos!"

"His mom is a whackadoodle!"

Why do I have the feeling that super-smart R.R.R. is going to be a pain in my behind for the rest of fifth grade and, probably, the rest of my life?

CHAPTER 8

Of course the new kid, Randolph R. Reich (I'd call him Triple R, but I already have a Triple H), is in Mrs. Kunkel's class with Trip and me.

"This is Randolph's first day here at Creekside," says Mrs. Kunkel. "I'm sure you'll all do your best to make him feel welcome."

I guess. If we have to.

E spends his day down the hall with the third graders in Ms. Tracey's classroom, where he's a stand-in for Maddie. In fact, as soon as E steps across the threshold into Ms. Tracey's room, Maddie takes control of his high-definition eyeball cameras. She also becomes his voice. E's artificial intelligence basically goes into sleep mode while Maddie takes over his robot body so she can participate in class. All from the germ-free comfort of her bedroom.

Meanwhile, in Mrs. Kunkel's classroom, we're doing math, and Mr. "I'm never wrong because I'm always Reich" is at the Smart Board.

"Okay, Randolph," says Mrs. Kunkel. "I give you two gray cats, two black cats, and two white cats. How many cats do you have?"

"Simple," says Mr. Smarty-Pants. "Seven."

All righty-o! I think Mr. Reich just scored his first wrong!

Trip and I are so happy, we slap each other a low five.

"Seven?" says Mrs. Kunkel. "Are you sure, Randolph?"

"Definitely," says Reich smugly, which, by the way, is how he says everything. He's so stuck-up he probably thinks that his breath wouldn't stink if he ate garlic knots dipped in garlic butter and sprinkled with garlic flakes.

GUESS WHO THE SMART BOARD WAS NAMED AFTER? THAT'S RIGHT. ME.

$\frac{1}{2} + \frac{2}{3} = \square$
$\frac{1}{2} + \frac{1}{6} = \square$
$\frac{1}{2} + \frac{3}{8} = \square$

"Let's try again, Randolph," says Mrs. Kunkel. "I give you two cats plus two cats plus two more cats. How many cats would you have?"

Reich rolls his eyes. "As I told you before, I would have seven."

"That's incorrect. Two plus two plus two equals six."

"Of course it does, Mrs. Kunkel. But I have another cat at home: Mr. Fluffles. Ergo, if you give me six more cats, I would have seven."

"Oh, I see," says Mrs. Kunkel, nodding. "I did not factor in your 'Mr. Fluffles.' My mistake."

Reich gives her another eye roll. "Clearly."

Wow. The teacher made the mistake, not Reich. I don't think that's ever happened in the history of school. Teachers all over the world have those special textbooks with all the answers printed in them. Teachers never, ever, not in a million years, make mistakes.

I wish I could say the same thing about my mother.

Because all of a sudden, the school secretary's voice is coming out of the ceiling speakers.

"Sammy Hayes-Rodriguez?" she says. "Please

report to Ms. Tracey's classroom. Immediately."

This can only mean one thing.

E must be on the fritz.

I hurry down the hall and, after knocking on the door, step into Ms. Tracey's classroom.

I see E, sitting in a shaft of sunlight near the windows. (It's Maddie's favorite spot in the whole room.) He's slumped sideways at the table he shares with four other third graders. The janitor is there with his toolbox, too.

"I think it's his batteries," says Ms. Tracey. "Maybe that's why Maddie didn't have her usual pep and energy today."

"Mom probably forgot to recharge him," I say.

"Can we recharge him here?" asks the janitor.

I nod. "We just have to plug him in."

I open a compartment on E's back.

It's empty.

"Um, Mom also forgot to send him to school with his recharging cable," I tell the janitor.

I hear a weak *BEEP-BLOOP-BEEP*.

That means E's running out of power. Even his backup batteries are almost fully drained.

"Mom?" he peeps. "Mom? Help meeeeeeee—"

And then—*KA-THUNK*—his head slumps forward onto his desk.

My bro-bot is officially out of juice.

CHAPTER
9

The janitor retrieves a rolling trash barrel from the cafeteria and we use it to wheel E up the hall.

"E ran out of power?" asks Principal Reyes when we bring E into the front office.

"Yes, ma'am."

"And Liz forgot to pack his charger cord?"

I just nod.

"Wow," says Principal Reyes. "That is so not like her."

That is so true.

Mom is the smartest person that I—and pretty much everyone in South Bend, Indiana—have ever met.

But like I've said, Mom's been messing up a lot lately.

Principal Reyes is a friend of my parents. She's in a rock band with my mother and father. They call themselves Almost Pretty Bad; I like to call them Not Very Good. The only decent member of the band is Jimi. Because he's a robot. That means he knows how to play his guitar so it doesn't sound like a cat when you step on its tail.

"This is a major mess-up," says Principal Reyes, gesturing toward the limp E. "Is your mother preoccupied with something else, Sammy? Is she working on some new breakthrough technology?"

All I can do is shrug and say, "I don't know."

Because lately Mom, the absentminded professor of robotics, has also been generally absent. I'm starting to think that's why our blueberries tasted like raisins this morning. She hasn't been updating the Breakfastinator's database on a regular basis like she usually does.

"Well, take good care of E, Sammy," says Principal Reyes as she heads into her office. "Give my best to your mom and dad. In fact, tell Liz to call me. If she's under a lot of stress, she might need a girls' night out."

I nod. Then I make a video call home to Maddie.

"It was so weird," she tells me. "We were in the middle of a spelling bee, and all of a sudden, E just cut out. He stopped sending me sound and video."

"His battery died," I tell her.

"Are you recharging him?"

"No. I mean, I would, but Mom forgot to pack his power cord in the cargo compartment. Add that to the list of her most recent goof-ups."

"Well, it's no biggie. I was winning the spelling bee but I'm sure we'll just pick it up tomorrow."

"Okay. I'm gonna call Mom. Tell her what's up."

"You up for more Spine Spinner Trivia when you get home?"

"Definitely. See you later."

Next I video-call Mom. She's in her workshop just behind our house.

And man, does she look like her brain is on some other planet.

"Hey, Mom," I say when her frazzled face pops up on my screen. "It's me. Sammy."

"Huh?"

"Your son."

"Huh."

All righty-o. Her mind is totally "in the zone." Which means it's not paying any attention to me.

"So, how come you're not at Notre Dame?" I ask.

She gives me a quizzical look. "What?"

"Notre Dame. You teach there?" I raise my arms Frankenstein-style, like one of her robots. "You're a professor of robotics. Remember?"

"Right. Robots. Can't talk right now, Sammy. Busy. Very important project. Very, very important."

"Okay, but, uh, well, you forgot to pack E's charger today and he sort of conked out in the middle of a spelling bee."

"Right. Okay. Thanks. I'm on it."

Then she must have hit the End Call button, because my whole screen goes blank.

Okay. Nice talking to you, Mom.

CHAPTER 10

Finally, I call Dad.

He's working on more illustrations for his graphic novel masterpiece, but when I tell him what happened to E, he puts down his pen and says he'll come pick me and E up right away.

"Uh, with what?" I ask.

"The SUV," he says. "It just needed its battery charged. The tow truck hauled it home and I just plugged it in."

"Same thing with E. His battery conked out."

While I'm waiting for Dad, guess who waltzes into the front office?

Yep. Randolph R. Reich. Mr. Know-It-All.

"Mrs. Kunkel wanted to make certain that you were all right," he tells me.

"Fine," I mumble. "My sister's robot just needs its batteries recharged."

"Probably because of that extra exertion in the drop-off lane this morning. Towing an SUV to the curb requires a great deal of power. The effort undoubtedly drained the robot's lithium cells dry."

"Maybe. I dunno."

"Of course you don't know. I, however, pride myself on knowing everything about anything. Was your robot, by chance, sitting in the sun when it experienced this rapid battery drain?"

"Yes," I admit.

He nods. "I thought so. Heat is a battery killer, Sammy. Each fifteen-degree rise in temperature cuts the life of a sealed battery in half."

Darn it. He's right again. "Thanks. I'll try to remember that."

"You should. Also, did you know that Alessandro Volta—the scientist who realized that electricity could be created by two different metals joined together by a moist intermediary—invented the battery in 1800? He used copper and zinc disks piled on top of each other, separated by cardboard soaked in brine, a brackish mixture of salt and water, also used when making pickles. The volt, which is the derived unit of electrical potential, is named after Signor Volta."

All righty-o. I've had enough.

"So tell me, Randolph: is there anything you don't know?"

Reich thinks about that. For maybe half a nano-second.

"Not really. Engineering, mathematics, the history of transportation, the meaning of abstract art. I know it all."

Luckily, that's when Dad comes to my rescue. We load poor E into the SUV and haul him home.

Halfway there, the electric SUV-EX starts sputtering. Again.

CHAPTER 11

We make it home!

We're actually pulling into our driveway! And then the SUV dies a slow, lurching death.

This time when it conks out, it also locks all the doors. We're trapped inside.

"Jiggle your door handle," says Dad.

I jiggle. "It's still locked."

Dad toggles the key. He presses the Start button. He pushes the Door Lock-Unlock button. He jabs the dashboard computer screen with his thumb, pounds a bunch of buttons in the center console with his fist, and tries to roll down the windows and open the sunroof. Nothing works.

Suddenly, the dead car starts talking. "Opening doors."

Dad and I look at each other and—quick! We grab our door handles half a second after the car says, "Doors locking."

We're stuck again.

"¡Qué pedazo de basura!" mutters Dad, basically calling Mom's latest and greatest invention a "hunk of junk."

As soon as he gets done calling it that, the Door

Lock knobs pop up. Then they pop back down. Up. Down.

It's like the SUV is messing with us.

"Keep your eye on the knob," says Dad. "Next time it pops up, pull your door handle. Pull it fast!"

So we both sit there. For three freaky minutes. Staring at the Door Lock knobs like they're toasters and we're waiting for our bagels to leap out. I'm starting to wonder if there is any food stashed in the glove compartment. We may be trapped in here for a while.

POINK!

Up pops my knob. I pull the handle.

I'm out!

Dad crawls ungracefully into the backseat. He's out, too.

"Now how do we open the back door to get E?" he wonders.

And that's when all the doors decide to automatically glide open.

"Have a nice day," says Soovee, chipper as ever.

"We need to talk to your mother about this," grumbles Dad. "Right now."

Yep. We're adding it to the list of Stuff That Mom Needs to Fix.

Dad pushes a button on his remote garage door opener. It activates Forkenstein—a headless robotic forklift Mom uses to haul heavy stuff around inside her lab. Forkenstein rumbles down the driveway on tank treads, sidles over to the SUV, and extends his lift arms to cradle E.

"Let's put you up on the rack and take a look at you," says Forkenstein, who now has a voice. Mom made him sound like the guys down at the corner gas station.

Dad and I follow the rolling bot up the driveway and into Mom's workshop, even though there is a DO NOT DISTURB! sign posted on the door. Mom is still busy working and doesn't notice as Forkenstein sets E down on a worktable and I plug him into the charger. His eyes glow a faint yellow as the electricity starts feeding his battery. When E is fully charged, his eyeballs turn a brilliant blue—the same color as Maddie's eyes.

"Liz?" says Dad.

She looks up from her desk and says, "Huh?" Again. Her dazed eyes tell me she's here but she isn't really *here*.

"The SUV stalled again," says Dad.

"Uh-huh."

"And this time it tried to trap us inside!"

"Huh."

"And E conked out at school," I remind her. "You forgot to pack his charger cord."

"Mm-hmm."

"Liz?" says Dad. "We really need you to spend a little more time in routine maintenance mode.

Robots are machines. A robot house can't run all by itself."

"Actually," mumbles Mom, "it probably could. There's a hierarchical protocol embedded in their control boards…"

She says a real long string of words that Dad and I don't understand. It's a lot of blah-blah-blah with lots of techno-mumbo jumbo.

But we both nod as if we get it.

"So, uh, you're going to fix everything?" says Dad. "E? The SUV?"

I add a couple of my own: "The Breakfastinator and the Groomatron?"

"Definitely," says Mom. "I'm on it. Later."

And then she goes back to focusing on whatever super-secret project has stopped her from focusing on anything and everything else.

Including her family.

CHAPTER 12

While Mom's mind is away, the robots will play. Actually, they will bump into each other, they will knock stuff over, and they will put way too much laundry detergent in the washing machine.

Mr. Moppenshine is the bot in charge of chores around the house. In addition to mopping, drying, and buffing the floor with his feet while simultaneously spritzing, spraying, and dusting with his hands, he's supposed to do the laundry. Pre-measured squeeze packs of allergen-free detergent plunk out of his nose tube whenever he bends over the washer.

Today he plunked six packets when he should've plunked one.

Meanwhile, Drone Malone, our flying bot—great

for recording high altitude YouTube videos and doing traffic reports—keeps banging into windows like a bird that thinks glass is just more wide-open space to fly through.

Then there's Blitzen, our super-aggressive lawn mower: he just scalped our entire front yard. Our grass isn't green anymore. It's just gone. We're also missing a birdbath. (I think Blitzen bulldozed it into the shrubbery. I hope there weren't any birds in it.)

Speaking of shrubbery, Hayseed, our gardener robot, isn't taking care of trimming the bushes out front because he's too busy digging holes in the backyard.

"Shoo-ee," he says, "Blitzen stirred up so much dang dust, the rabbits are digging holes six feet in the air." He sinks his shovel into the ground again.

"Well, um, why are *you* digging holes?" I ask.

"Well, I noticed that the dang Fooderlator was all out of chicken again," he says.

The Fooderlator is the robotic machine in the kitchen that automatically makes our dinner on nights when Mom and Dad are too busy to cook or we don't just go out and grab a pizza (which is what we do on most nights when Dad's supposed to cook).

"So I thought we ought to raise our own chickens," Hayseed goes on, leaning on his shovel handle. "So, I'm gonna plant me some eggs—just as soon as the Breakfastinator has some of *them* again."

I guess if the backyard starts smelling like rotten eggs, I'll know why.

Trip bikes over after school to witness the chaos and confusion.

"Wow. This reminds me of the week after Christmas when my brand-new remote control car went wacky," says Trip. "I think some of your robots' motion detectors aren't detecting motion anymore."

Yep. More routine maintenance that Mom has let slip while she concentrates on her super-important, top-secret, high-tech breakthrough project, leaving me, Dad, Maddie, and the robots to take care of ourselves.

CHAPTER 13

I'm able to use the Robo Control app on my phone to stop the bots from bumping into each other and the walls like Roombas gone wild.

"That should keep them functioning till morning," I tell Trip.

"And then what?" he asks.

"Hopefully, Mom will come out of her workshop for fifteen minutes and program their work assignments for the day. It's something she usually does every morning, before any of the rest of us are even up."

"Cool," says Trip. "So, what are you guys having for dinner tonight?"

Trip has a look on his face that tells me a) he's hungry and b) he wouldn't mind eating dinner at our house tonight.

My guess is his mother is making her famous Tofurky casserole. I had it at his house once. It tasted like a wet cardboard box stuffed with carrots.

"I'm not sure what we're having," I say.

"Well, whatever it is," says Trip, "it's got to be better than what my mom's cooking tonight: Brussels sprouts surprise."

"What's the surprise?"

"That there's nothing in it but Brussels sprouts."

We head into the kitchen, where Dad is futzing with the Fooderlator.

"Hello, Mr. Rodriguez," says Trip. "What are you making for dinner?"

"Black bean chicken with rice," Dad answers. "Steak fajitas, turkey burritos with fresh fruit salsa, *empanadas con ropa vieja,* and, for dessert, apricot pinwheel cookies!"

Trip is practically drooling. Me too.

"Really?" I say. "You're making all that?"

"No," says Dad. "I doodled it on my sketch pad.

Made me so hungry, I couldn't think about Ninja Manatees anymore. So, I came in here to whip something up. Let's see what we have to work with…"

"Um, Dad?" I say. "Weren't you supposed to go grocery shopping this week?"

"Yes, Sammy, but I'm way behind on my book and coming up on a major deadline, so I was hoping your mom could cover me this week, even though, *technically*, it was my turn. But she couldn't go shopping because she's doing something majorly important and not doing any of her chores or even brushing her teeth or combing her hair on a regular basis. Then the SUV started acting up, E's battery ran down at school, I had to stop Blitzen from plowing the backyard, Mr. Moppenshine started dusting my face..."

I just nod.

Mom and Dad usually do stuff as a team. If one of them gets busy, the other one picks up the slack. But now, both of my parental units are crazy stressed and burning the candle at both ends, which, sooner or later, will scorch your fingers and make you scream, "Youch! Who lit this thing at both ends?"

I check out the refrigerated bins that store raw ingredients for the Fooderlator to turn into delicious gourmet meals. They're all basically empty, like Dad said, except he missed an ancient peach with a bruise in the shape of Ohio.

"That is so gross," says Trip, peering over my shoulder at the rancid groceries littering the otherwise empty food drawers.

We go over to the fridge and stare at its bare shelves. Dad opens a cupboard. We have one box of Cream of Wheat and some saltines.

"So, you guys want to eat dinner at my house tonight?" asks Trip.

Dad looks interested. "What's on the menu?"

"Brussels sprouts surprise."

He stops looking interested. "Oh. No thanks."

"I have an idea," I say. "Let's eat out!"

"Great idea!" says Trip.

"We can bring something home for Maddie, too."

"Perfect," says Dad. "How about pizza?"

"Pizza would be fantastic!" I tell him.

"I love pizza," says the voice of Maddie, who, I guess, has been listening to our conversation upstairs, over her intercom. "But not delivery. Papa Pasquale's, please."

"You've got it," says Dad, grabbing his car keys. "Let's go pick up a couple of pies!"

"Woo-hoo!"

Yes, Trip and I are both pretty excited and extremely hungry.

But Dad doesn't dash out the back door.

"Slight problem," he says, keys in hand, feet not moving.

"Oh, right," I say.

"What?" asks Trip.

"Our brand-new car," says Maddie over the intercom. "It's dead. In the driveway."

So we stay in the kitchen and listen to the empty Fooderlator hum.

"Well," I say, "we could always bike it."

"That's true," says Trip. "I rode mine over here."

"I've got mine," I say.

"What about me?" asks Dad.

"You can borrow E's," I say. "He won't need it until his battery is fully charged."

So the three of us pedal over to Papa Pasquale's Pizzeria.

People in the neighborhood stand on their porches and gawk at us when we ride home juggling three big pizza boxes. They think we're weirdos.

And you know what? They're kind of right.

But for once, it's kind of fun being a weirdo.

CHAPTER 14

Maddie is feeling well enough to join us downstairs in the kitchen for dinner.

To make sure she doesn't pick up any stray germs, Trip has to put on a sterile mask that he flips up every time he bites into his pizza slice. Then he flips it down to chew and swallow. It sort of makes him look like a bunny rabbit nibbling carrots.

LET ME SLICE THE PIZZA. I'M DRESSED LIKE A SURGEON!

Dad and I don't have to wear the protective gear. Because we live with Maddie, she's already been exposed to all of our germs.

"Tomorrow," says Dad, "I promise I'll go to the supermarket. Right after I finish inking in a few panels my art director needs ASAP. I also have to do a few rewrites for my editor. But they're minor."

"You think maybe Mom could cover for you tomorrow?" I ask.

"No, Sammy. Whatever she's working on right now is very important."

"What is it?" asks Trip.

Dad shrugs. "She won't say."

I notice that Maddie is avoiding everybody's eyes by playing with her spinach and mushrooms. Yes, that's what she likes on her half of the pizza. Me? I go with pepperoni.

"Hey, speaking of super-important scientific stuff…" says Trip.

"I know, I know," I tell him. "We need to work on our science project."

"Mrs. Kunkel wants a progress update," says Trip. "Tomorrow."

"Fine. Just be sure to bring your dad's electric

tire pump. Our ball is so big, it would take us all day to blow it up by mouth."

"No problem."

"You guys?" interrupts Maddie, sort of sheepishly. "I think I need to say something."

"What's up, hon?" asks Dad.

"I might know what Mom's working on. Why she's kind of letting everything else slide..."

"Really?" I say. "What is it?"

Maddie hesitates. "It's for me."

"Awesome," I say, because, like I told you, I love my little sister. If Mom is doing something to help Maddie, I'm all for it. "What exactly is she working on?"

"I'm not sure," says Maddie. "She just told me she needed to 'disappear' for a little while. But if things went the way she hoped they would, I'd be thrilled with the results."

"Wow," says Trip. "That is so awesome."

"Wonder what it is..." says Dad.

"Well," I tell him, "we can't ask her. You know how Mom gets when she's working on a big idea. 'Talking about it can jinx it.' That's what she kept saying when she was working on E."

"Wait a second," says Trip. "Do you think Dr.

Hayes is making Maddie another, brand-new robot?"

Maddie smiles. "Well, I *did* tell Mom that I wish I could sing with my friends in the Creekside Elementary Choir."

"And E is totally tone-deaf!" I say, because I tried to teach him how to sing along with the radio, and it was a disaster. McFetch, the robo-dog, howls better than E sings. E can't rap, either. Trust me. We tried that, too.

"It would be so cool if Mom could make me a karaoke-bot," says Maddie. When she gets happy like this, her blue eyes really sparkle. "A machine that I could sing through!"

OH, SAY, DOES THAT STAR-SPANGLED BANNER YET WAVE...

WOW! I CAN SHATTER GLASS WHEN WE HIT THE HIGH NOTE COMING UP!

"Well, guys," says Dad, smiling at Maddie, "how about we pick up the slack for Mom a little longer? I'll restock the Fooderlator tomorrow and make sure the SUV is ready to roll."

"I'll make sure E has his charger cables for school," I say. "And that he doesn't sit in the sunshine too long."

"And I'll make everybody peanut-butter-and-banana sandwiches for lunch!" adds Trip.

"Fine," I say with a laugh. "Just make sure your mom doesn't surprise us by slipping a few Brussels sprouts in with the bananas!"

CHAPTER 15

After dinner, I head out to the garage to box up the gear that Trip and I will need for our science project check-in with Mrs. Kunkel.

I fold up the clear plastic sphere, then pack it in a bag. I stuff the bag into a cardboard box and tape it shut. We don't want our competition seeing what we're up to until the very last second.

"Hello, Sammy!"

E joins me in the garage. He looks and sounds like his old self. His eyes are glowing bright blue again.

"Are you fully charged?" I ask.

"Yes," he says. "I am, as you say, ready to rock!"

"It's great to have you back, E," I tell him. "And don't worry. I'll make sure we take your charger cable to school tomorrow."

"Excellent. I don't want to let Maddie down. I believe she was in the middle of spelling *something* when I conked out."

"What was the word?"

"*Something.*"

"You don't remember?"

"Yes, it was *something*."

I get it now. "Oh. S-o-m-e-t-h-i-n-g."

"Correct." E gestures toward the cardboard box. "Are those the materials for your science project?"

"Yep."

"If I may ask, what are you and Trip working on?"

"Can you keep a secret?"

"Of course. My memory data is protected with hacker-proof encryption."

"It's a cool invention for Maddie."

"Aha," says E. "Like mother, like son."

"Yeah. I guess. I never thought about it like that. See, Trip and I don't think it's fair that Maddie is, more or less, trapped in our house all the time. So we decided to build her an all-terrain bubble ball so she can go outside with her friends!"

E looks confused.

"I first got the idea at the grocery store. You know those vending machines that give you small toys inside plastic capsules?"

E nods.

"Well, they kind of reminded me of a hamster ball I saw at a pet store. And then thinking about the hamster ball reminded me of these water-walking balls I saw at Trip's lake house last summer. They're huge, like, six feet wide, and made out of clear, strong plastic that floats on top of the water. You just blow them up with a tire pump, step inside, and—*BAM!* You can walk on water!

"So, I started thinking: What if we could turn the water-walking ball into an anywhere-walking ball? What if Maddie could climb inside a sterile ball and go for a walk in the park with all her friends, without having to worry about germs or stepping in dog poop?"

"Fascinating," says E. "Definitely a hypothesis worth exploring."

"Exactly. So for our science project, Trip and I—"

I'm about to explain the whole thing when I hear angry voices coming from the backyard.

Angry *robot* voices.

CHAPTER 16

Most of Mom's robots are huddled under an oak tree in our backyard, having some kind of secret meeting.

They don't sound happy.

It's almost like a robot rally. Everyone has a complaint.

"It's utterly shambolic," says Geoffrey, the butler-bot with a British accent. "We're being neglected whilst Dr. Hayes fiddles with whatever bits and bobs she has in her workshop."

"Mom is so mean and totally unfair," whines Brittney 13, a robot that Mom programmed to imitate the emotions of a teenager. Constantly. Nonstop. We're talking 24/7.

I TELL YOU WHAT, FELLERS: WHEN A BUZZARD SITS ON A FENCE AND STARES AT YOU, IT'S TIME TO GO SEE A DOCTOR. AND THAT'S EXACTLY WHAT WE NEED. SOME DOCTOR BESIDES DR. ELIZABETH HAYES TO MAKE OUR CIRCUITS HUM AGAIN!

"I don't wanna play here anymore!" says Four, popping its detachable pacifier thumb into its mouth. Mom created Four to act like a four-year-old. Don't ask me why. Four doesn't do much around the house except scribble all over Maddie's coloring books when she's not looking.

"We need to do somethin' 'bout this," says Hayseed. "And soon! I'm already feelin' as confused as a fart in a fan factory."

E goes over to the grumbling bots. "If I may..."

"E!" says Geoffrey. "Good to see you up and about, old chap."

"Thank you. And to be quite honest, I didn't need Mom's help to restore my functions to their fully operational state. Sammy did it for me."

"I did?" I say, stepping out of the shadows so all the other robots can see me.

"Yes," says E. "You plugged me into my charger."

"Oh, right." I shrug. "It was no biggie."

"Well, what the heck is goin' on that's so gall darn important that Dr. Hayes couldn't just plug you in herself?" demands Hayseed.

"Yeah," grunts Blitzen. "She forgot to give me my lawn mowing coordinates this morning, so I plowed the front yard. Coach Rodriguez benched me for it."

"She also failed to program my feather duster settings," says Mr. Moppenshine. "I destroyed two lamp shades and a chandelier today!"

"Can you program yourselves to program yourselves?" I suggest.

"We are, indeed, artificially intelligent," says Geoffrey. "However, we still require human support and input."

"We need Mommy!" blurts Four. Then it pops its thumb back into its mouth hole.

The others pick up on its demand. "We need Dr. Hayes!"

Forget the robot rally…this could be a robot revolution!

"Dr. Hayes is working on a top-secret, highly classified project," says E, raising his voice slightly. He's trying to calm the other bots, all of whom are pumping their fists in the air and saying stuff like *"¡Viva la revolución!"*

"Like I said, what is she workin' on that's so dad-gum important?" demands Hayseed, still jabbing a pitchfork in the air.

"I do not know," says E. "But I can only assume that it might yield enormous benefits."

"Benefits for, like, who?" demands Brittney 13.

"All of humanity," says E. "And most importantly, Maddie!"

Immediately, the other robots stop chanting and pumping their fists and stabbing the sky with the pitchforks.

"Maddie," they sigh in unison.

It's true. The robots in our house are as crazy about my little sister as I am.

"So let's make a deal," I say. "Let's give Mom the time and space she needs to work on whatever it is she's working on. And Dad is pretty tied up with his book deadline right now. So for the next few days or weeks or however long it takes, I promise I will get up extra early and program your daily operational routines." I wiggle-waggle my phone. "I have an app for that."

The robots start nodding and mumbling their agreement.

"Jolly good idea," says Geoffrey. "Thank you, old bean. Now back inside, everybody. We all have work to do. Chop-chop."

"Um, like, what exactly are we supposed to do?" asks Brittney 13.

"Take the night off," I say grandly. "You'll receive your new assignments in the morning."

They all happily *WHIR* and *CLICK* and *SCHLUNK* back into the house.

Except E. He stays with me.

"This is quite commendable of you, Sammy. To step in like that. Your mother and father are both so busy, you are the logical choice to take over day-to-day operational supervision."

"Thanks," I say. "But E: There's only one way this is ever going to work. You've got to do it with me."

E nods. "Agreed. I have the same app hardwired to my motherboard."

"Awesome!"

We shake on it. Starting tomorrow, the whole house of robots will be run by E...and me.

Hoo-boy. Wish us luck.

I think we're going to need it.

CHAPTER 17

The next morning, E and I both wake up two hours earlier than usual.

If we're going to be in charge of the house's "robotic operations," as E calls it, we need to hit the ground running.

While E boots up and completes another charging cycle, I grab a quick shower. This time, when I step out, the Groomatron blasts me with a typhoon of oven-hot air. It's so toasty, it doesn't just chap my lips: it chaps my whole face like it's a pizza crust.

"Is there some problem?" asks E as he steps into my bathroom.

"Yes! It's baking me to a crackly crunch!"

E holds up his palm and shoots some sort of reddish light at the Groomatron. It shuts down. "Mom equipped me with a universal infrared remote control. I can power on or off any bot in the house. I can also change TV channels and fast-forward DVDs."

"How do we fix this crazy thing?" I ask him when the Groomatron stops whirring. "I don't want to shut it down."

"I have an idea."

"Good. Because I have burnt eyeballs."

"I suspect the Groomatron, as well as the other robots in this house, are in a rut, Sammy."

"Huh?"

"They have all been programmed to do one thing and one thing only. Their routines have become too, for lack of a better word, routine."

"But they're machines, E. They're designed to do the same, specific job over and over and over again."

E nods. "What you say is correct. For machines. But do not forget: all of the robots engineered by your mother and her associates at the University of Notre Dame have been equipped with artificial intelligence. We are able to learn, change, and adapt. For instance, I can now say 'Yo, bro' when conversing with you because I have learned that such expressions are preferred to the more formal 'Greetings, Samuel' that I was originally programmed to recite."

"O-kay. So how do we get the Groomatron to adapt back to being a hair dryer again?"

"Perhaps by allowing it to function as something else for a period of time. It is my theory that if we send electrical surges into underutilized circuits in all the various robots' motherboards, the knowledge and skill sets related to their primary tasks will also increase exponentially."

"Wait a second. You're saying the Groomatron will be a better hair dryer if we let it do something else for a while?"

"Exactly."

"So that's your plan? Shake things up? Get all of the bots to do things they've never done before?"

"Yes. For instance, instead of drying your hair, what if the Groomatron functioned as your personal adviser?"

"Huh?"

E scoots forward and, using his clamper claws like socket wrenches, twirls a few knobs to open up the Groomatron's outer casing.

"Some simple rewiring coupled with a revised binary command code should do the trick."

One of his fingers becomes red-hot like a soldering iron. Another one flicks tiny microprocessor switches up and down.

A few *ZITZ*, *WHIR*, and *CLICK*s later, the Groomatron looks like it always does. But then it starts talking.

"Goooooood morning, Sammeeeeee Haaaaayes-Rodreeeeeeguez!"

The box sounds like a morning deejay on the radio.

"No need to pack a rain cane today, but be sure to grab a jacket or light wrap. We're looking at temperatures in the sixties, dipping down to the fifties later on tonight..."

It gives me sports scores, my horoscope, wardrobe tips, a rundown on all my homework assignments, and a word of the day: "Potentiality:

a capacity or ability for growth and fulfillment." All very enthusiastically.

In other words, E is right. The Groomatron is happy doing something besides blowing hot air at my hair.

E scoots around the rest of the house and reprograms all the bots. Today they're all getting new jobs.

CHAPTER 18

When Maddie wakes up, E has already repro-grammed the Breakfastinator in her room.

"With these new objectives," says E, "will come increased efficiency when the bots return to their primary functions."

"Um, are you, like, one hundred percent certain of this?" I ask.

"Sammy?" says Maddie. "No scientist is ever completely certain of the outcome when they start an experiment."

"So that's what this is?" I say to E. "An experiment?"

E nods. "Founded on some very sound theoretical thinking. Much like your science project, Sammy."

My science project! I have to remember to stop forgetting about that.

The Breakfastinator starts executing its new task: sorting Maddie's socks.

"So who do you guys have making breakfast?" Maddie asks.

"Hayseed. Consider him part of the new farm-to-table dining trend."

Hayseed scoots into the room toting two plates filled with leafy green things. "I done made y'all some vittles."

"It looks like a salad," I tell him.

"I reckon it does at that."

"What is it?" asks Maddie. "Because we usually have oatmeal or cereal or Greek yogurt…"

"Cain't get Greek yogurt straight from an American farm lessen it's a dairy farm with Greek cows, I reckon. These here are dandelions."

I stare at the plate of weeds. "Seriously?"

Maddie isn't too thrilled, either. "Salad? For breakfast?"

"It is quite customary in Japan," says E because he can tell that, so far, his "experiment" isn't going well in the breakfast department.

"I think I'll just split a peanut-butter-and-banana sandwich with Trip," I say.

"Nuh-unh," says Hayseed. "You need to eat you some greens. Some yellows, too. Them dandelion flowers look deeeee-licious."

Maddie and I choke down our greens (and some yellows). When E and Hayseed aren't looking, I pull a granola bar out of my backpack and toss it to Maddie.

"Thanks, Sammy," she whispers.

"Breakfast is the most important meal of the day," I tell her. "Except, I guess, in Japan, where they probably eat seaweed and raw fish in the morning, too."

"That's on tomorrow's menu!" says Hayseed.

Great. I had to open my big mouth.

Instead of playing our usual morning trivia, Maddie and I get quizzed on the differences between deciduous and evergreen trees. I feel bad for my sister, but I decide to head to school early.

E and I say good-bye to Maddie and head downstairs. We're biking to school today because the SUV-EX is still dead in the driveway. Blitzen, the lawn mower-bot who used to be a middle linebacker on Notre Dame's robotic football team, is under the electric vehicle, banging and slamming stuff because, well, that's what linebackers do.

"Come on, engine!" he grunts. "Give me everything you've got or I'm pulling you out of the game!"

I glance into the backyard and see Mr. Moppenshine dusting the grass.

"Since Blitzen is on motorized vehicle maintenance duty today, I put Mr. Moppenshine in charge of lawn care," says E. "His new command is to keep the grass looking tidy at all times."

"Great. He might be finished with the backyard by Christmas."

I don't know about E, but I'm getting the feeling that this job-swapping experiment wasn't the best idea...

CHAPTER 19

As we're grabbing our bikes out of the garage, my phone chirps. I don't recognize the number in the caller ID window but I answer it anyway.

"Hello?"

"Hello, Sammy. This is your personal valet."

I don't believe this. The Groomatron—my automatic hair dryer—is calling me.

"I just wanted to remind you that you need to show your science project progress at school today. So be sure to pack up all the equipment you're going to need."

"Um, I can't take it to school with me on my bike. The basket isn't big enough to hold all the stuff."

"Might I suggest you stow it in the SUV-EX? Blitzen informs me that he'll have the car up and running in no time at all."

"Come on, Soovee!" I hear Blitzen shout from underneath the car. "You can do it. Just give me two more!" More banging, clanging, bashing, and thumping.

"Let's do as Groomeo suggests, bro," says E.

"Groomeo?"

"That's the new moniker I chose for myself," says the Groomatron over my phone. "I'm more than a grooming machine, Sammy. I am your personal assistant!"

All righty-o. I'm starting to wonder if the idea behind E's bot experiment is just not very good or actually cuckoo-loony.

"I've already texted your father," the Groomatron continues. "I reminded him to bring Maddie's robotic dog with him when he drops off the rest of your science project supplies this afternoon."

That's good. McFetch is a big part of our planned demonstration.

"Thanks," I say.

E blinks his blue eyes like he's waiting for me to say something else.

"I mean, thanks, Groomeo."

"You are quite welcome, Sammy. And might I just add, I am enjoying the challenge of my new responsibilities."

"Me too!" hollers Blitzen. And then he starts hammering more metal against metal.

E and I load the boxes for my science project into Soovee and bike off to school.

We have a pretty good bro-bot chat along the way.

"Mom is under so much stress," I say. "How could building a singing robot take up so much of her time and attention?"

"Perhaps she is working on something much more complex than what Maddie suggested."

"Sometimes I just wish Mom would tell us what she's working on."

"But scientists need the freedom to fail, Sammy. And failure is something almost everybody prefers to do in private."

"You're right. When I get a bad grade on my report card, I sure don't like showing it to Mom and Dad."

"We must continue to give Mom the space and time she needs to complete her experiment, whatever it might be. For her sake as well as Maddie's."

Halfway to school, Trip joins us on his bike.

"Hi, guys!" he says. "I figured your car might still be dead and you two might be riding your bikes to school again, and guess what? I was right!"

"Did you remember the electric air pump?" I ask him.

"Yep. But where's everything else?"

"Packed up in Soovee," says E.

"The one that's still dead in your driveway?" says Trip.

"Don't worry," I tell him. "Groomeo promised me that Dad will deliver everything this afternoon."

"Cool," says Trip. "So who's Groomeo?"

"My talking hair dryer."

"And personal assistant," adds E.

"Neat!" says Trip. "I want one of those."

I'm tempted to say he can have mine. But I don't want to hurt E's feelings.

"You're sure you guys packed up everything?" asks Trip. "You didn't forget anything?"

"Nope," I say because I double-checked all the boxes after we loaded them into the SUV.

But I do have a nagging feeling that I've forgotten *something*—I can't remember what. Until after lunch.

Because that's when Mrs. Kunkel reminds me.

CHAPTER 20

After lunch, we come back to our classroom from the cafeteria and Mrs. Kunkel is writing Mom's name on the whiteboard at the front of the room.

"Boys and girls," she says, "today is a day I have been looking forward to for several months! We have a very special visitor—a real scientist to help put us all in the mood for our upcoming science fair."

Uh-oh. I think we have something else to add to the list of Stuff That Mom Is Supposed to Do but Isn't.

"Today," says Mrs. Kunkel, "Sammy's mother, Dr. Elizabeth Hayes, a brilliant robotics professor at Notre Dame, will tell us about all the incredible robots she has designed and the work she's doing on building robots of the future!"

The whole class oohs and aahs. Then they start applauding.

Well, everybody except Randolph R. Reich.

"This is so cool!" says Trip. "Did your mom ride her own bike to school? Did that forklift robot, Forkenstein, haul her here?"

I just smile. Nervously.

When the cheering and the applause finally stop, Mrs. Kunkel turns to me.

"Has your mother arrived, Sammy? I hope she brought a few of the robots with her."

"Um, I, uh…" I want to crawl under the desk and hide until it's time for high school.

Mrs. Kunkel and the whole class stare at me. Except Randolph. He's smirking.

Finally, I just blurt it out: "I think she forgot that she's supposed to be here today."

"Really?" says Mrs. Kunkel. "I called her yesterday to remind her."

"Well, she's been kind of busy and distracted lately. I think she's working on a top-secret project."

"After that preposterous electric SUV idea, what foolish invention is it this time?" sniggers Randolph. "A submarine with open windows? A helicopter that doesn't fly?"

There's a knock on the classroom door. My hopes soar as high as Drone Malone on a windy day. Maybe Mom remembered after all!

The door opens.

It's…*Dad?*

"Sorry we're late," he says. "Our robots took longer to fix the car than we thought they would. Hi,

Sammy! Hi, Trip! We put your science experiment boxes in the gym."

Oh yeah. I forgot he was dropping them off for me.

"Thanks, Mr. Rodriguez," says Trip.

"Is, uh, Mom with you?" I ask hopefully.

"No, but I saw her calendar and noticed that she was supposed to come speak to your class today. I'm sorry, Mrs. Kunkel. Liz can't leave her lab right now. But since E has all our robots switching jobs, I thought I'd bring a substitute speaker for you guys."

And in walks Geoffrey, our very British butler-bot.

Oh no. Of all the awesome robots in our house, why'd he pick *Geoffrey?*

"See you at home, Sammy. Wish I could stay, but I've got that darn deadline to deal with. Forkenstein will come pick up Geoffrey in an hour. Buh-bye!"

My father is such a lucky guy. He gets to leave before Geoffrey starts talking.

"Greetings and salutations, children. I am, indeed, a robot. That means I am an autonomous electromechanical machine guided by software and electronic circuitry…"

He is also, to use another technical term, a big bore.

"Dr. Hayes is, as you've heard, busy at home doing research. Research is what scientists do when they don't really know what they're doing, eh, what?"

"Well said, old bean," shouts Trip.

Everyone stares at Trip. Then they stare at me.

Hoo-boy.

This is so embarrassing I may not climb out from under my desk until I go to college.

CHAPTER 21

When Geoffrey finally finishes (thirty minutes after he started), Mrs. Kunkel's room looks like a kindergarten class during naptime.

Everyone has their head on their desk, taking a quick snooze.

Even Mrs. Kunkel!

Thankfully, the bell signaling the end of the day rings.

"Does someone need to answer that?" asks Geoffrey. "Hello? Is that the phone or is someone at the front door?"

No one is listening to him. They're all streaming out the door, heading to the gym to set up their science projects so Mrs. Kunkel can see our progress.

They're also laughing their heads off at me and my family, and poor Trip, too, because he's a friend of me and my family.

"That butler-bot is such a joke!"

"Sammy's whole family is a joke!"

"I guess *butler* is another word for *boring*."

Randolph R. Reich marches up to me. "Well, that was extremely tedious," he says. "The next time your mother is too busy to fulfill her obligations, please find someone—or some*thing*—more interesting to take her place."

Once again, he's right! The guy is batting a thousand. He never makes a mistake. How does he do that? I seem to make a mistake every time I wake up and roll out of bed.

"By the way," says Randolph, "I can't wait to see what you and your chum, Harry Hunter Hudson, have come up with for the science fair. I'm sure it will be just as dazzling as your butler's scintillating and sparkling oration."

All righty-o. I think he's being sarcastic. Then again, I could be wrong. Like I said, I make a lot of mistakes.

Trip and I head into the gym and find the boxes Dad delivered. McFetch starts happily wagging his robotic tail and gives us a couple eager yaps when his incredible sense of smell picks up our scent. I'm guessing he smelled Trip first. If you eat peanut-butter-and-banana sandwiches every day for lunch, you develop a very distinctive odor.

"Hey, boy," I say, patting McFetch on the head, right where Mom gave him a touch sensor. "You ready to go to work?"

He yaps *"Yes!"* I think.

Trip hooks up his electric tire pump and blows up our clear plastic water ball. When it's inflated to its huge six-foot diameter, I tug open the zipper, place McFetch inside, and seal the ball up tight.

Mrs. Kunkel comes over, carrying a clipboard.

"All right, Sammy, Trip. What have we here?"

"This," I say proudly, "is a prototype for the Germ-Free Freedom Ball, a completely sanitary mobile isolation chamber. Now kids with compromised immune systems can go outside, anywhere and everywhere other kids can go."

"We built it for Sammy's sister," adds Trip.

"Fascinating," says Mrs. Kunkel. "How exactly does it work?"

"Perfectly," says Trip, snorting back a laugh. "If we do say so ourselves."

"Allow us to demonstrate," I add.

Mrs. Kunkel steps back. I pull out McFetch's favorite squeaky ball and heave it across the gym floor. It rolls to a stop under the far basketball net. McFetch yaps and starts furiously churning his legs toward it.

The Freedom Ball starts spinning! It rolls up the hardwood like it's on a fast break to do a dunk.

"Very well done, Sammy, Trip," says Mrs. Kunkel. "Your invention could provide Maddie with all the protection she needs to freely leave your home."

"Exactly!" I say.

All the other kids (except R.R.R.) start cheering Trip and me. We slap each other a high five. It feels great to be a brilliant scientist.

For almost a whole minute.

CHAPTER 22

Turns out one of the other kids in Mrs. Kunkel's class, Josh DeBardeleben, is doing his science project to determine which brand of bacon has the most fat.

He's set up a line of hot plates and sizzling frying pans so he can cook six different kinds of bacon, pour the drippings into a measuring cup, and see which one generates the most grease.

The second he starts his experiment, the whole gym smells like the Wakin' to Bacon Diner, a place that serves nothing but eggs and bacon, BLTs, bacon-wrapped bacon balls, and bacon burgers. McFetch starts sniffing the air inside his plastic ball. I guess the zippered flap isn't as tightly sealed as we thought. Besides, Mom gave the robo-dog extremely complex odor sensors.

The plastic ball rolls across the slick gym floor like a bowling ball on a skating rink. I chase after it, but it's slipping and sliding every which way.

Our wildly out-of-control science project is careening toward the other side of the gym, rushing toward Josh DeBardeleben's bacon station. But first, it has to go around Lena Elizabeth Cahill, who's setting up a three-panel poster board exploring which candy causes Diet Coke to explode the most.

Lena has an open two-liter bottle, and when she sees McFetch's giant hamster ball rolling straight at her, she panics and drops a whole roll of Mentos into the jug.

Brown foam starts spewing all over the place— especially when our sterile bubble ball slams into Lena's table and knocks it over. I slip on the wet floor and get soaked in sticky Diet Coke...right in front of the cutest girl in school!

When Lena's card table topples to the floor, one of its pointy metal legs spears our ball, puncturing the plastic. McFetch rips the hole open even wider and escapes to go gobble bacon. Our bubble is officially burst.

I pick up our Freedom Ball, which is now a shriveled heap of crumpled vinyl covered with Diet Coke lava. "I guess we have some issues to work out on how to control the ball's direction," I mumble to Mrs. Kunkel.

"I'd say so," says Mrs. Kunkel. She ticks a few boxes on her clipboard. "Not very sterile or hygienic, boys. I applaud the good intentions behind your, eh, invention, but I think you two need to head back to the drawing board and start over to achieve your desired results."

"Yes, ma'am," we both mumble as Lena Elizabeth Cahill yells, "Sammy Hayes-Rodriguez is an idiot!"

Things can't get much worse. Or so I think.

At the far end of our row of tables, Randolph R. Reich announces, "If you're quite finished doing damage control with those two, Mrs. Kunkel, I am ready to initiate my demonstration."

She bustles up the line to see R.R.R.'s entry for the science fair.

Trip and I shuffle behind her to check it out, too.

Having eaten all of Josh DeBardeleben's science experiment, McFetch goes to sit under our table and squeak his ball.

I sort of wish I could do that, too.

CHAPTER 23

"**W**hat's your hypothesis, Randolph?" Mrs. Kunkel asks Reich when we reach his exhibit.

The guy is pounding his fist into a baseball mitt that has all sorts of LEDs blinking in the pocket and laser beams shooting out of the webbing.

"It's not actually a hypothesis, theory, or supposition, Mrs. Kunkel. It is a proven fact."

"You've already tested your concept?"

Reich scoffs at that. "Of course. I never leave room for error. In fact, that is the guiding principle behind my latest invention: the Laser-Assisted Magneto Mitt. In baseball, particularly at the Little

League level, there are far too many 'errors.'"

"They're part of the game," I say.

"Correction. They *used* to be part of the game. With my new and improved glove, plus a few simple alterations to baseballs, such as the installation of miniature GPS trackers at their core, a fielder should be able to catch anything hit his way. Allow me to demonstrate. Coach Stringer, if you please? Swing away."

At the far end of the gym, Coach Stringer tosses up a ball and taps it into a line drive.

The ball changes its course in midair and sails into Reich's glove.

"I borrowed much of my technology from NASA and the Pentagon," Reich says smugly, because that's the way he says everything.

Coach Stringer turns to face the far wall so his next hit will fly *away* from Reich. He flips up another ball, swings, and launches a soft pop-up.

It should land, like, thirty feet away from Reich.

It doesn't.

It curves hard to the right, like a guided missile, and plops into Randolph's waiting mitt.

"B-b-but your invention will ruin baseball," stutters a horrified Trip. "No one will ever score a run. After nine innings, every game will end up tied at zero-zero. They'll have to go into extra innings that last to infinity!"

"Not necessarily," says Reich, snagging yet another line drive. "Home runs, because of their trajectory and height, will continue to soar beyond the range of the L.A.M.M."

"The what?" I ask.

"The Laser-Assisted Magneto Mitt."

"Right," I mumble. "The L.A.M.M.—another way to spell *lame...*"

Trip and I grumble some more as Reich snags each and every ball Coach Stringer puts into the air.

Everybody else, Mrs. Kunkel included, is oohing and aahing.

Reich's science project is a definite hit.

Ours? A big miss.

Or, to put that in baseball terms, a total error.

CHAPTER 24

Unfortunately, E's experiment is going just about as well as our science project.

When we bike home, we discover that Mr. Moppenshine is still in the backyard, feather-dusting tree leaves.

I CLEAN THE COBWEBS OFF THE BRANCHES, BUT THIS TINY INSECT CREATURE KEEPS MAKING NEW ONES!

HAYES-RODRIGUEZ

STOP

"I'm going to clean and disinfect all the flying creatures next," he announces. "Some of them appear rather dingy."

"What flying creatures?" I ask.

He points at a robin.

"That's a bird," I tell him. "You can't spray disinfectant on birds."

"Why not?" demands Mr. Moppenshine. "They're filthy, as if they've been digging around in the dirt. That one even has a worm in its mouth."

Things inside aren't any better. Blitzen mowed a path down the center of the carpet in the living room.

"I finished fixing the SUV," he tells E. "But I miss mowing. The feel of clippings tickling my belly. The rumbling roll downfield toward victory. The joy of trampling everything in my path. Tomorrow, I've got my eye on a few bath mats."

"Sammy, is that you?" Maddie yells from upstairs. "E? I need help!"

We hurry up the stairs and into Maddie's room. The air smells like burnt rope. Maddie is kind of cowering in the corner, pointing at the Breakfastinator.

"It started cooking my socks!" Maddie informs us.

"Now serving a tasty fried knee-high," drones a computerized voice as the Breakfastinator shoots out wads of balled-up, smoldering socks. "Now serving an argyle omelet!"

Even Matt, the educational exercise game, is acting up. Literally. It's standing upright in the center of the room. "I'm tired of taking everything lying down. I'm too smart to be a rug. I want to be a game show host on TV!"

"E? What new task did you give to Matt?"

"Foot massaging. Perhaps he thought it was beneath him."

Even McFetch is acting up.

He eats Maddie's homework—even though robot dogs don't need to eat anything except electricity.

"Your theory about giving the robots new tasks isn't working," I tell E.

"I beg to differ," he replies. "All the bots seem ready to return to their original routines with renewed vigor and determination."

"If they don't trash the house first!"

"I will make the necessary adjustments to their motherboards," says E. "Meanwhile, I advise that you and Trip should make the necessary adjustments to your science project."

"You heard about that, huh?"

"Yes, Sammy. My social media feed reported that everybody at Creekside Elementary was talking about your science project and Randolph R. Reich's magnificent magneto mitt, but for very different reasons. But do not despair. As you see by the misbehaving bots, all scientific experiments encounter slight bumps along the road to progress."

"Except Randolph R. Reich. He never makes a mistake."

"For now," says E. "But perhaps that will prove to be his biggest mistake."

"Seriously? Doing everything perfectly is a mistake somehow?"

E actually grins. "We shall see, Sammy. We shall see."

CHAPTER 25

Okay. I need to talk to Mom.

I know she's super busy working on her top-secret project, but she's a scientist. I need one of those—to help me with my *science* project. Dad's a great artist and all, but he's pretty terrible when it comes to fixing stuff. He can't even make a Pez dispenser work right.

I tiptoe into Mom's workshop. When she's in the zone, you definitely don't want to startle her. She'll jump right out of her lab coat.

The walls are covered with math equations that I don't think even Albert Einstein would understand. There is an entire row of robotic arms squirting goop into glass trays and then shuffling them down the line for different goop squirts. Tools and machinery parts are *everywhere*. There's even a wrench poking out of Mom's mug of day-old coffee.

The place is a wreck.

And Mom looks worse.

Mom sees me. I think. Her eyes have a glazed and distant look.

"So, Mom," I say. "I know you're super busy, but, well, I need to talk to you about something extremely important."

"This isn't really a good time, Sammy. Can't your father help you?"

"No. Not really. Because this is a science question and, in case you haven't noticed, Dad isn't much of a scientist. He can't even mix hot water and tea bags to make tea. You, on the other hand..."

"I, on the other hand, am extremely busy, Sammy, working on two breakthrough ideas. One will improve the lives of every human on the planet. The other will, more important, significantly improve your sister's life."

"This is all something for Maddie?" I say, gesturing at the jumble of clutter surrounding us.

"Most of it."

"Well, what are you building her? A karaoke robot?"

"Where did you get that idea? No, it's something much more meaningful."

"Like what?"

"I'm not ready to talk about it, Sammy."

I roll my eyes. We've all heard this so many times. "Because talking about it can jinx it."

"Exactly. And both of these projects are too important to jeopardize with premature speculation."

"So why are you working on *two* projects at once?"

"Ideas come when they come, Sammy. We cannot dictate the timing of our inspirations."

I nod.

But inside? I hate to admit it, but I'm sort of mad.

How come improving Maddie's life or the lives of everybody else on the planet always comes first?

What about my life? I live on the planet, too! Am I just supposed to muddle through everything without any help from my genius mom?

I mean, if Trip and I had her brain on our team, we could crush Randolph R. Reich at the science fair. She could use one of her "inspirations" to make our giant plastic hamster ball fly like it was fired out of a cannon. And I'd put a magnet in it so it'd shoot right for Reich's batty baseball glove—while he was wearing it.

We could totally make him crash and burn. Hand him his first mistake. Not that Mom ever would. But we *could*.

I stuff my hands in my pockets and slouch out of Mom's workshop. I don't think she even notices me leaving. She's too busy working on something to save the planet and make Maddie's life better, while mine keeps on getting worse.

I find Dad. He's at his drawing board, putting the finishing touches on his masterpiece.

"Looking good, no?" he says.

"Looking good, yes!" I tell him.

"Almost done." He puts down his pen. Rubs some of the ink off his fingers with a blackened cloth. "I need to scan in these drawings, but I can do it later. Now, what's on your mind, Sammy? You have that look on your face."

I THINK THIS
← IS THE **LOOK**
HE MEANS.

"The science project," I tell him with a sigh. "All that stuff you dragged to school for me and Trip."

"Right. How'd that work out?"

"Terrible."

"That bad, huh?"

"Worse. Lena Elizabeth Cahill may never speak to me again. Not that she's ever spoken to me before…"

"Ouch."

"Our whole idea stinks."

Dad nods. "I know the feeling." He points to the wire basket near his drawing table. It's filled with crumpled balls of sketch pad paper.

"So, what do you do when your first idea is horrible?"

"Easy," he says with a smile. "I come up with the second idea."

CHAPTER 26

I try to follow Dad's advice.

Hey, with Mom so busy, it's the only advice I'm going to get.

"I need a new idea for the science project," I tell E as we're biking to school the next day.

"And it seems I need a new idea for restoring order to the house of robots. You were correct yesterday when you said my idea was not working."

"Well, maybe we can help each other."

"An excellent suggestion, Sammy. We can brainstorm. Free-associate. Bounce ideas off each other. Spitball concepts and see which ones stick to the wall."

"You know about spitballs?"

"Yes, Sammy. After all, I have been going to school for a while now."

"Cool. Can I go first? That way, if you like my idea, I can tell it to Trip when we meet up with him on the corner."

"Please proceed."

"Okay. I was thinking of how we could give Maddie more control over the direction of the plastic ball. Have you ever seen that car the Pope drives around in? The one with the big bubble in the back?"

"I am googling it on my hard drive now."

"You can do that and ride a bike at the same time?"

"Indeed. Your mother pulled out all the stops when she engineered me."

Because she was building E for Maddie, is what I'm thinking because, yes, I'm still sort of jealous or mad (or maybe both).

"Okay," I say. "What if we took Mom's idea for an electric car and mashed it up with the Freedom Ball? We could put the ball around an electric golf cart to keep it sterile, and Maddie could ride around inside."

"It might work," says E, sounding like he thinks it never actually *will* work.

"Okay, I got this next idea from Mr. Moppenshine when he was trying to clean the birds in our backyard. What if Mom could build a walking can of disinfectant spray? A spray-bot! The Spritzatron 1000! It could walk behind Maddie and constantly fog the air around her with a cloud of germ-killing spray!"

"Of the two," says E, "I prefer the Maddiemobile."

"Yeah," I say. "Me too. Trip and I just need to find a golf cart we can borrow."

Trip is waiting for us at the corner on his bike.

"Why do we need a golf cart?" he asks.

"You heard that?"

"Yeah. You talk really loud when you're on your bike."

"It's for the science project."

"Oh. Well, we don't have a golf cart, but we do have a riding lawn mower that pulls a little green wagon."

"That might work…"

"Outdoors only," says E. "Otherwise, there could be a serious carbon monoxide problem."

"Hey, speaking of serious problems," says Trip, "are you ready to go one-on-one with Randy Reich in your debate?"

"Huh?"

"Today's Debate Day, remember? Mrs. Kunkel chose you and Randy to go up against each other first thing this morning."

Good ol' Trip. Still saying the wrong thing at exactly the wrong time.

Like reminding me that I have to debate Randolph R. Reich, the guy who never, ever makes a mistake.

CHAPTER 27

All righty-o. This terrible week just won't end. Since I just found out it's Debate Day, there's absolutely no time for me to listen to E's ideas about how to restore order among the robots at home. Which is a pretty important conversation, because some of our household helpers have gone completely rogue. For instance, last night, Hayseed told everybody that he planned on planting corn in the middle of Interstate 90.

"If Dr. Hayes is too dadgum busy to pay attention to us, we should pursue other projects," he told all the other robots when they were holding another one of their protest rallies in the backyard. "They got them that long stretch of green what goes down the road 'tween the east- and westbound lanes."

He was talking about the median strip. On the Indiana Toll Road! "There ain't nothin' growin' there now but weeds and wildflowers. Well, fellers, I mean to cultivate that narrow strip of land. Sure, it might be as hard as putting socks on a rooster, but it'll sure beat settin' around here not knowin' which way is up."

I'm starting to think that the best solution for our robot revolt is to pull all their plugs. But then I'd have to do all the dishes.

Anyway, E says good-bye and *ZHOOSH*es down the hall to the third-grade classroom.

Trip and I hurry into Mrs. Kunkel's class to hear what today's debate topic might be. Mrs. Kunkel has Debate Day once a week: two of us stand in front of the whole class and argue yes or no on a certain question.

Last week, Trip and Lena Elizabeth Cahill debated "Should schools stop selling chocolate milk?"

The week before that, the topic was, "Should parents be able to take their kids out of school for vacations?"

I sure wish mine would.

And I wish we were on vacation today.

Because even though my mother thinks this whole debate idea of Mrs. Kunkel's is genius, I *hate* getting up in front of the class—especially since you don't know what you're going to be debating about until five minutes before you have to start arguing for or against something.

"Sammy?" asks Mrs. Kunkel ten seconds after the bell rings. "Randolph? Are you ready for your debate topic?"

"Of course," says R.R.R., straightening his tie.

It's a bow tie today. Makes him look even more like a miniature banker.

"I guess," I mumble.

"Here is your question: Perfection—is it possible?"

She writes the question on the board. "Randolph, you will be arguing *for* perfection as a goal."

"Wonderful," he says, rubbing his hands together gleefully.

"Sammy? You will be arguing *against* perfection as a possibility."

"Of course he will be," cracks Reich. "Imperfection is how Sammy rolls."

The whole class (including Trip, that traitor) chuckles.

"Save it for the debate, Mr. Reich," says Mrs. Kunkel.

"Gladly."

"You both have five minutes to prepare. And while they do that, I want the rest of you to spend the time doing your silent reading."

I scribble down a few ideas, but the five minutes are up in what feels like five seconds.

Randolph R. Reich goes first.

"I'd like to start with something the legendary football coach Vince Lombardi always told his team: 'Perfection is not attainable, but if we chase perfection, we can catch excellence.' But if perfection isn't possible, we wouldn't bother chasing it. And as you know, I do chase it and frequently attain it. Therefore, Mrs. Kunkel, fellow students, I say perfection *is* possible, and should always be our goal. Never let puny mistakes hold you back from being all that you can be. Always reach for the moon, ladies and gentlemen." He stretches out his hand dramatically. "Even if you fall short, you will land among the stars!"

The classroom erupts with applause.

"Very well argued, Randolph," says Mrs. Kunkel. She turns to me. "Samuel?"

I go to the front of the class and stuff my hands into my pockets.

"Well, uh..." I look over at Randolph. "People always say, 'Nobody's perfect.' Then again, they also say, 'Practice makes perfect.' I sort of wish they'd make up their minds. So, in conclusion, I'd have to say that perfection isn't possible unless you practice a lot. And who wants to go to practice all the time, since, like I said, nobody's perfect? The end."

I don't get applause. Just blank stares. Maybe I should've added a few hand gestures. I drag myself back to my seat.

"Thank you, Sammy," says Mrs. Kunkel. "That was very...interesting."

The class votes on who made the best case

for their side of the argument. R.R.R. wins. By a landslide. Even *I* vote for the guy.

What can I say? The guy is perfection in a coat and tie. Even his hair is perfectly parted and combed—and he doesn't have a Groomatron in his bathroom.

Then again, neither do I.

Mine went on strike this morning.

He said being my personal assistant was "boring." Listening to my debate speech, I might have to agree with him.

I also think I'm in big trouble.

Señora Goldstein just came into the room. And I don't like the way she's looking at me.

CHAPTER 28

Señora Goldstein is the teacher who gives us Spanish lessons for an hour, three times a week. Sometimes we sing the taco song while she strums her guitar.

"I need this signed, Señor Hayes-Rodriguez," she says, handing me a graded homework paper. "By *both* of your parents. *Su madre y su padre. ¿Comprendéis?*"

"*Oui,*" I say, even though I think that might be French.

I turn the paper over and see the big, fat, red fifty-two. It's circled three times. There's a frowny face next to it that sort of matches the frowny face Señora Goldstein is giving me now.

I don't bother sharing this bad news with E on the bike ride home. He has enough bad news of his own.

Seems like Drone Malone attacked our neighbor's bird feeder this afternoon. He thought the sparrows were stealing the birdseed inside. E seriously needs to reprogram all the bots in the house before they do some major damage.

I show my fifty-two to Dad first.

"*¿Cómo es esto posible?*"

Yep. He says the same thing I did because we both speak Spanish very well—he's the one who's been teaching me since I was a baby. It means "How is this even possible?"

"I don't know. I guess I had a bad day."

"A fifty-two? What will your grandparents say?"

Yikes. *Mis abuelos.* They'll be so disappointed.

"Do we have to tell them?" I ask.

Dad shakes his head. "No. We all have bad days. We all make mistakes."

"I know," I say. "That's why my pencil has an eraser."

Dad grabs his chunky art eraser. "Here. Use mine. It's bigger."

He signs my homework, up near the fifty-two. He draws a frowny face wearing a sombrero. "Now go take this to your mother. Ask her to sign it, too."

"But she's so busy…"

"She's never too busy to be your mother, Sammy. Go. *¡Date prisa!* I need to finish this drawing."

I shuffle out to Mom's workshop. There are even more math equations and formulas scribbled everywhere. For some reason, the electric SUV-EX is parked in the middle of the floor. Mom is tinkering with the domed thingy on its roof.

"Um, Mom, hate to disturb you," I say, limply waving my sheet of Spanish homework.

"You already did."

"Right. I just need you to sign this."

"What is it?"

"Something from school. You can sign right under where Dad did."

She climbs down from the SUV and hunts for a pen.

"You see, I sort of failed a Spanish assignment. Terrible, huh?"

Mom nods like she's listening, but she doesn't seem to hear a word I say.

"I mean, we speak Spanish here at home."

"Mm-hmm," she says as she bites the cap off her pen.

"Even McFetch the robo-dog understands Spanish commands, so how'd I end up with a fifty-two? It's so weird."

"Hmm," is all Mom says. Then she signs. No questions asked. No fuss, no muss.

Phew. That's a relief.

Sort of.

I bet if Maddie got a fifty-two on a Spanish assignment, Mom would drop whatever she was doing and start building her a bilingual robot that was also a mariachi singer.

I look at my homework. Mom's signature is all wrong—she just scribbled a wavy line, like she couldn't even take the two seconds to write her name for real.

That does it.

I blow up.

"You are the worst mother ever!" I scream.

I storm out.

Leaving Mom red-faced and sputtering in her workshop.

CHAPTER 29

Inside the house, there's another disaster.

It seems the robots sent Brittney 13—our teenage emoticon of an automaton—to the grocery store to do the shopping. She came back with four frozen Hot Pockets (chicken with cheddar and broccoli—yuck!), plus copies of *Tiger Beat, Girls' Life, J-14, Teen Vogue,* and six other magazines with bright pink covers.

"They were, like, right there at the checkout counter," she gushes. "Omigod. I just had to have them all. They're so sick!"

"You mean the magazines are ill?" asks E. "If they are contagious, they could prove hazardous to Maddie's health."

While I explain to E that *sick* sometimes means *awesome,* Hayseed nukes our dinner in the microwave.

"I don't appreciate this dadgum machine's attitude," he mutters, slamming the door shut. "Always beeping behind my back. Thinkin' it's so dadburn smart because it can pop popcorn *and* bake potatoes. Reminds me of E. Thinks the sun comes up just to hear him go cock-a-doodle-doo."

"I beg your pardon?" says E. "Are you implying that I am, somehow, conccited, arrogant, stuck-up, and/or smug?"

"Of course I is!" hollers Hayseed like I've never heard him holler before. "Everybody knows you're Dr. Hayes's favorite. Why, I wish I had half the brains she gave you."

"If you did," says Geoffrey the butler-bot snobbishly, "you still wouldn't know a widget from a whangdoodle."

Hayseed doesn't like the sound of that. "I tell you what, Mr. Snooty Pants from France..."

"England!"

"Same difference."

Yep. All of Mom's robots are starting to get a little snarky with each other.

"I have an idea," says Dad when he finally braves a step into the kitchen, which is cluttered with clanking, catty contraptions. "Let's eat upstairs! In Maddie's room."

"Awesome idea," says Maddie. "No robots allowed."

The three of us grab our Hot Pockets out of the microwave, slap them on paper plates, and dash up the stairs to Maddie's room. The Breakfastinator is shut down now, recovering from sock shock.

"One more panel and it's done," Dad tells us, buzzing about his new book. The walls of Maddie's room are papered with Dad's drawings because Maddie loves looking at them. I do, too, but he didn't put any in my room. I guess I could *ask* Dad to print out some art for me, but, well, it always means more when your parents think to do nice stuff like that on their own.

Wow. *Am I mad at Dad, too?*

Am I really this jealous of Maddie, my best friend in the whole world?

I'm starting to feel terrible because, don't forget, she's seriously sick.

And then I start to feel even worse.

I want to tell Dad and Maddie about my argument with Mom, but before I can, E escorts Mom into the room, carrying her Hot Pocket on a paper plate.

"Thought I'd join you guys for dinner," she says.

"Grab a seat," says Dad, offering her his.

Mom sits down and doesn't say a word to me.

Pretty soon, nobody's talking. We're just listening to each other chomp and chew our Hot Pockets. Nobody even yelps when the molten cheese inside the Hot Pockets scalds the roofs of our mouths (which they do every time anybody bites into one).

E tries to break the silence.

"How nice that you all could be together for dinner!" he chirps. "There's nothing like good food and good conversation. And this is nothing like good food or good conversation."

We all just stare at him.

He's funny. But right now, none of us are in the mood to laugh.

CHAPTER 30

Good news: the next morning, it's raining out! Wait. That's not the good news. The good news is that the electric SUV-EX is still up and running, so Trip, E, and I don't have to ride our bikes to school in the rain!

"Please fasten your seat belts," says Soovee's dashboard. "And kindly remove your hands from the steering wheel, Mr. Rodriguez."

Dad chuckles. "How exactly do you expect me to make turns? With my knees?"

"Your assistance is not required this morning, Mr. Rodriguez. Perhaps you'd like to watch a short movie?"

A cartoon is projected on the windshield in front of Dad's face.

"Soovee?" I ask. "Did Mom make it so you can drive yourself?"

"Correct."

"This is so cool!" says Trip.

"Yesterday, Dr. Hayes mounted a range finder to my roof housing a 64-beam laser."

So that's what she was doing when she was too busy to look at my rotten Spanish homework.

"This laser allows me to generate a detailed 3-D map of my environment," Soovee continues. "I will take that map and instantaneously overlay it on top of high-resolution, real-time traffic maps and produce all the data models I need to drive myself, and you, safely to school."

"But what if the police see me not driving?" asks Dad.

"No worries," purrs the car. "Mom also tinted the windshield. You can see out, but no one can see in. Why, you could fully recline your seat and take a quick nap."

Okay. I know what I want our new science project to be: Soovee—the self-driving electric car!

"Sit back, relax, and enjoy the ride," says the dashboard as we whir backwards out of the driveway, make a gentle turn, and head up the block toward an intersection.

"Stop sign!" Dad shouts.

"I see it, sir," Soovee states calmly. "Kindly remove your foot from my brake pedal. Given the wet pavement, you are applying too much pressure and could send us into a skid."

"Oh. Sorry." Dad raises his hands in surrender and settles into his seat.

"Isn't technology marvelous?" says E. "Especially when it frees humans to pursue more important tasks. Now, instead of driving, you can work on your sketches, Mr. Rodriguez. Right here in the car."

"But I like driving," says Dad. "I do a lot of thinking and daydreaming when I drive."

"They call that distracted driving, sir," says E. "The roadways will be far safer without it."

"I guess..."

Five minutes after we leave home, we ease into the school driveway. Lena Elizabeth Cahill is on safety patrol duty again. I start waving. I *so* want her to see me in my autonomous automobile, which is what you call a car that can drive itself.

"Look, Lena!" I shout after I roll down the window. "No hands!" I point at my dad behind the steering wheel.

Dad rolls down his window and waves at Lena with both hands.

"Our car is driving all by itself!" I holler happily for all the world to hear. Or, at least, all of Creekside Elementary.

And, of course, that's when the SUV bids us a

pleasant "Good-bye," dims all its lights, and dies.

Right in the middle of the drop-off lane.

During rush hour.

Again.

Yep. This has to be the worst year of my life.

CHAPTER 31

That morning in Mrs. Kunkel's class, right after everybody, including Trip, is finished laughing at me, my family, and our autonomous automobile (which, if you ask me, needs an Auto Correct button), I get another lousy grade to add to my collection.

It's a sixty-nine on a pop quiz we took the other day. That's not as bad as my fifty-two on the Spanish homework. In fact, I think a sixty-nine is a D. Maybe a D plus.

But the pop quiz was in science. Science used to be my best subject. And not because Mom helps me with my homework! I just like science. Well, I used to. Lately? Not so much. Maybe because science is what's keeping my mother holed up in her workshop instead of being a mother. To me, at least.

"Well done, Randolph," Mrs. Kunkel says when she hands R.R.R. his test. "No one else scored a one hundred and three!"

One hundred and three? How is that even possible?

Reich looks pretty happy with himself. "I suppose no one else decided to elucidate on how a condenser can change water vapor into a liquid?"

"No. They just knew that condensation is what makes the mirror fog up when you take a hot shower on a cold day. Except Sammy. He said that was caused by 'low-lying clouds.'"

Yep. That's what I wrote. I was having an off day.

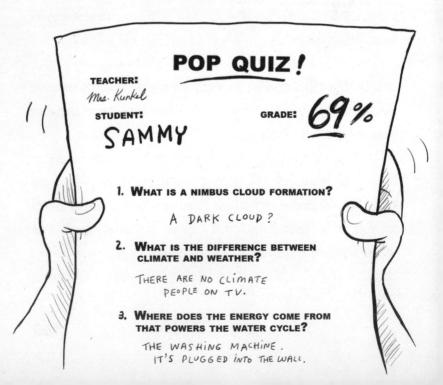

POP QUIZ!

TEACHER:
Mrs. Kunkel

STUDENT:
SAMMY

GRADE: **69%**

1. **WHAT IS A NIMBUS CLOUD FORMATION?**

   A DARK CLOUD?

2. **WHAT IS THE DIFFERENCE BETWEEN CLIMATE AND WEATHER?**

   THERE ARE NO CLIMATE PEOPLE ON TV.

3. **WHERE DOES THE ENERGY COME FROM THAT POWERS THE WATER CYCLE?**

   THE WASHING MACHINE. IT'S PLUGGED INTO THE WALL.

After school, Dad picks E and me up in a white van I've never seen before.

"It's a rental," he tells us. "My book is due to my editor. I can't afford to spend half my day calling tow trucks for that stupid SUV."

Great. Now Dad doesn't sound like Dad. Maybe he's joining the robot revolt, too.

As soon as we're home, E heads for Mom's workshop. "I want to build some prototype controllers for the rest of the robots," he says. "I must try to correct my previous reprogramming missteps."

But Mom kicks him right out.

"She says she is at the most critical stage of her experiment," he explains, his eyes dimming a bit. "We are not to disturb her."

Ha! What else is new?

Before dinner (Brittney 13 picked up some kind of frozen pancakes wrapped around sausages on Popsicle sticks), I head into Maddie's room.

"Why are you so sad?" she asks.

"I don't know. I guess because I'm all of a sudden flunking all the subjects I used to be good at. Spanish. Science. And those are just the ones starting with *s*."

"Well, have you been studying? Did you read your textbooks and do your homework?"

"No. Not really. I've been too focused on our science fair project. It's taken over my brain. Trip and I might've bitten off more than we can chew."

"What are you guys trying to do? Be the first kids to land on Mars?"

Maddie makes me smile. She's good at that.

"I wish," I say. "It might be easier. No, I have this idea about making your life more fun."

"You're doing a project for me?"

"Yeah. I didn't want to tell you, in case it didn't work…"

"You're just like Mom!"

E said that, too. "I guess you're right. I thought if I talked about what Trip and I were doing—"

"You'd jinx it!"

"Exactly. We're trying to find a way for you to be able to horse around outside with your friends. Maybe even play soccer with 'em."

"That would be so cool! What'd you come up with?"

"Nothing so far. Well, nothing that actually works. I'm like Mom that way, too."

"Well, don't give up, Sammy," says Dad, coming into Maddie's room with another drawing to hang on the wall. "Stick to it. Just like your Mom always does. That's why, when she's close to an answer, she keeps herself locked up in her workshop. So come on, have a little faith. She'll find what she's searching for and then she'll be back at the dinner table eating pancakes on a stick with the rest of us."

That makes us all laugh.

Until we hear an explosion.

The three of us run to the window.

We see Mom staggering out of her workshop, in a cloud of smoke!

CHAPTER 32

Mom spends the entire night in her workshop—probably trying to fix whatever it was that blew up.

Meanwhile, inside the house, the robots are all kind of blowing up, too. They're not exploding, but they're seriously misbehaving. I didn't think it could get much worse, but I was wrong. Instead of doing what robots are supposed to do—help humans—they've decided to do the exact opposite: make life miserable for everybody.

I'm pretty sure one of them filled my shampoo bottle with glue this morning and shrunk my bath towels into washcloths while I was in the shower.

I'm not pointing fingers here, but Groomeo the Groomatron sure looks proud of himself.

The Breakfastinator is back to making breakfast, but it has a new surprise recipe "courtesy of Trip's mother."

You guessed it: *Brussels sprouts surprise.*

With a side order of scrambled cauliflower. Have you ever smelled overcooked vegetables first thing in the morning? Don't do it. Unless you already have some of that sawdust gunk that school janitors use everywhere to soak up puke puddles. You'd need it.

"This is bad, Sammy," says Maddie as we both stare at our early morning vegetable platters. "Worse than that dandelion salad and the seaweed combined."

"Yep. And I have a feeling it's only going to get worse."

I, of course, am correct.

Dad is way too busy finishing up his graphic novel and scanning images into his computer to do anything about the out-of-control bots. And E is outnumbered.

"You were designed to be better than this," E tells Geoffrey the butler-bot, who is busy unscrewing all the lids on every ketchup jar, mustard bottle, and saltshaker in the house so they'll fly off when one of us humans tries to use them.

"I grow weary of roboticists orchestrating our every move," says Geoffrey. "I have sensors and actuators and, by jingo, I am not afraid to utilize them! Now if you will excuse me, I need to go to the bathroom."

"No, you don't," I say. "You're a robot. It's one of

the best things about being a machine! You never, *ever* have to go to the bathroom."

Geoffrey doesn't listen to me or E. He scoots into the closest bathroom and starts fiddling with the showerheads so they'll fly off and surprise us, too.

Meanwhile, outside, Hayseed is leaving squishy "organic surprises" all over the place. In the lawn. In my bike basket. Even in my gym shoes, which I sometimes keep on the back porch because they stink so bad. Well, now they smell even worse. Don't forget, Hayseed's our gardener. He has sacks filled with cow manure to use for his pranks.

I know that I could easily shut off each of Mom's robots so they'd stop misbehaving. With a flick of a switch, they'd power down and just be silent hunks of metal in the garage, and my sneakers would be free of cow poop. But I don't want to shut them off.

Because I understand what they're feeling.

These bots are only upset because they don't think Mom is paying enough attention to them.

That's right. They kind of remind me of me.

CHAPTER 33

E and I are going to be late to school.

Drone Malone won't let us anywhere near our bikes, and we already missed the bus.

He's hovering near the garage carrying two very droopy, very heavy-looking balloons. This can't be good.

"I don't think those balloons are filled with water," I tell E.

"I agree. I believe Hayseed loaded those breakable inflatables with the same substance he loaded into your gym shoes."

Gross.

"I'm leaving my gym shoes at home and skipping PE today," I tell E.

"You might also wish to go back inside and adjust your hairstyle," E suggests.

"Can't. The Groomatron slipped glue into my shampoo. Groomeo has gone goofy-o."

"Today I am ashamed to call myself a robot," says E with what sounds like a very human sigh. "We were designed to process information and compute the best way to complete our tasks. We were engineered to serve. We were not meant to be this selfish."

"I guess Mom made you guys a little too human,"
I say.

"Perhaps."

Suddenly, the intercom speakers all over the
house, even near the back door, play this loop of
marimba music.

It's the ringtone from Maddie's iPhone.

"May I have your attention, please," says Maddie
over the intercom.

"This is Maddie.
I am so sorry to
hear that so many
of you guys are
feeling kind of lousy right
now. Trust me. I know what
that's like. Every time my
fever spikes and the paramedics on the ambulance crew
come to take me to the hospital,
I just feel lousy.

PLEASE STAND BY FOR AN INSPIRATIONAL PEP TALK TO RIVAL THOSE GIVEN BY KNUTE ROCKNE, ARA PARSEGHIAN, LOU HOLTZ, AND ALL THE OTHER FAMOUS FOOTBALL COACHES IN NOTRE DAME HISTORY!

"But you guys always make
me feel better. Geoffrey? You always tell my visitors
to take off their shoes, put on sterile masks, and
rub sanitizer on their hands. Mr. Moppenshine?
If it wasn't for you—cleaning and scrubbing and

disinfecting everything—I'd be even more of a prisoner in my own home. And McFetch? What would I do without you? You keep me company, all day long. My life's a lot less lonely with you in it.

"And yes, E, my new bro-bot, has been a huge help. Thanks to E, I get to go to a real school for the first time ever. And as much as I like Trip and Sammy, it's been fun making some other real, human friends.

"But when all is said and done, you robots are my family. I hardly ever leave or even go outside— unless I'm on my way to the hospital. So, you guys, I just want you to know you mean more than the world to me. You *are* the world to me! My whole world!"

Before Maddie finishes her little pep talk, there isn't a dry electromagnet, capacitor, servo, or solenoid in the house.

"In conclusion," Maddie says over the intercom, "I want to do more to help. Maybe I can be the new mini mom for our house of robots. I'm here all the time— even when I go to school. If you need something, just let me know and I'll do my best to get it for you. And when it comes to our real mom, because think about it: Dr. Elizabeth Hayes is everybody's

mother in this house, except, of course, Dad's, and Trip's, if he's here—"

"I'm not," shouts Trip, who just rode his bike up our driveway. "I mean, I wasn't. Not when you were saying all that mushy junk about your mom, even though I kind of heard it out on the street because the volume dial on your intercom is cranked all the way to eleven or something..."

Maddie laughs. "Thank you, Trip. So, like I was saying, when it comes to Mom, we all just need to keep the faith. What she's working on has to be extremely important or she wouldn't be working on it so hard."

All the robots start nodding.

And then Geoffrey leads them all in a rousing song.

"For Maddie's a jolly good human! For Maddie's a jolly good human!"

While they finish their hip hips and hoorays, E and I grab our bikes and head off to school with Trip.

Luckily, Drone Malone is too busy cheering for Maddie to drop a wobbly poop balloon on my gluey hair!

CHAPTER 34

All righty-o.

Maddie's early morning pep talk seems to have done the job!

When E and I come home from school, all the other bots are humming along, completing their tasks with speed and efficiency. The lawn is so lush and green, it reminds me of a golf course.

"I done resodded the whole thing," explains Hayseed.

"And then I mowed it," adds Blitzen.

Mr. Moppenshine buffed and polished all the gleaming glass and chrome and countertops in the kitchen. The stainless steel refrigerator door is so shiny, you can use it as a full-length mirror. Which Brittney 13 does. Constantly.

Even McFetch is on his best behavior. He's teaching himself some new tricks by watching video clips of that winning dog act from *America's Got Talent*.

"They are all using their effectors quite effectively," E says proudly.

"Huh?" I say.

"Sorry. Effectors are devices, such as a gripper, tool, or laser beam, that allow robots to affect things in the outside world."

"Cool," I say. "Who has the laser beam?"

"Drone Malone."

"He should fly over to Trip's house someday. His cat goes crazy chasing laser pointers."

"I will pass along the suggestion, Sammy."

Seems Maddie's pep talk got to Dad, too. He totally restocked the Fooderlator.

"Tonight, we feast on grilled shrimp tacos!" he announces as he bops a few buttons. Yes, the Fooderlator can flame-broil stuff. Mom picked up some of its parts from a nearby Burger King.

The wafting aroma of barbecue shrimp is enough to lure Mom out of her lab. She joins us at the table for the first real family dinner in what seems like forever.

"This is delicious, Noah," she tells Dad.

"It wasn't me," he says modestly. "Your machine did all the work."

"Just like we always do, Mum," adds Geoffrey with a bow as he serves Mom her third helping of shrimp tacos.

"Is there any more salsa?" Mom asks.

And with the help of Brittney 13, who stops posing in front of the refrigerator door long enough to open it, Drone Malone airlifts a jar of cilantro-lime salsa over to the table.

Yep. Everything is running like clockwork. Just like a house full of mechanical taskmasters should. Even our family seems like it's back to normal. I guess Mom and I have called a truce, because we try our best to be nice to each other again.

When dinner's done, we play a fun game of Scrabble—humans only. The bots know too many words.

"This is great, you guys," says Mom. "Thanks for picking up my slack. I am pleased to report that my dual projects might be nearing completion."

"Might?" I say.

"Well, I'm still hitting stumbling blocks on the most important project."

"What are you working on?" I ask. "Maybe we can help."

Mom smiles and cocks an eyebrow. "Sammy?"

"I know, I know. If you tell us, you might jinx it."

"If I may inquire, Mum," says Geoffrey, "what exactly is a jinx?"

"It's the name of Trip's cat," I say, because, well, it is.

E, who is our resident vocabulary whiz, takes over for me.

"A jinx," he explains, "is an unseen force that is thought to bring bad luck or misfortune."

"Is that what Trip's cat does?" Maddie asks me.

"Nah. Mostly she just licks herself and hacks up hair balls."

Now everybody is laughing—including the robots equipped with humor detectors.

"Dang, that's a regular knee-slapper," says Hayseed, poking his head through the kitchen window. "I'd slap my knee but I'm afraid I might dent it."

"You guys?" says Mom, smiling. "I promise that everything is going to be okay."

And you know what?

Everything *is* okay.

For a few hours, anyway.

I'm sound asleep up in my room when, all of a sudden, I hear this incredible *KABANG!*

It's followed by a *CRACKLE-CRUUUNCH*.

It's louder than my alarm clock, which, by the way, is telling me it's two o'clock in the morning. Literally. The thing is a robot, and when its motion detectors sense that I'm looking straight at it, it *tells* me the time.

I ignore the clock and race to the window.

What now? Another explosion in Mom's workshop?

Nope! When I pull back my curtains, I see that Soovee, Mom's autonomous automobile, has crashed right through the garage door!

Splintered wood and twisted metal are scattered everywhere. All of it is from the demolished garage door. The SUV, sitting in the driveway, isn't dinged, dented, or even scratched. Mom must've made it out of something indestructible.

"Who would like to go for a ride?" Soovee chirps as it blinks and flashes all its various LEDs. The thing looks like one of those Christmas trees with the hyperactive lights. "I would like to go for a ride. Who would like to go with me? I am equipped with new cartoons and video games…"

Mom climbs out through the jagged hole in the splintered garage door. She's still in her lab coat. Guess she went back to work after our shrimp taco dinner.

"Liz? Are you okay?" Dad comes racing out the back door in his robe. E's right behind him. No robe.

E is carrying a first-aid kit the size of a suitcase. We have a bunch of them stored all over the house,

and not just for Maddie. We need them handy for Mom's experiments, too.

I grab my robe, hurry out of my bedroom, and hustle down the hall.

Maddie sticks her head out her door. "Is everything okay downstairs, Sammy?"

"I think so," I holler over my shoulder as I round the landing and hit the stairs. "Mom's autonomous automobile just tried to turn itself into an automatic garage door opener."

"Did it work?"

"Nope. Not really."

When I reach the back porch, most of our robots are already out in the driveway, trying to assist Mom and Dad.

Soovee's midnight ride has also woken up half the neighborhood. There are a lot of people in pajamas and robes standing on the sidewalk in front of our house, gawking at all the robotic activity in our driveway.

"What was that horrible noise?" asks Mrs. Pingle, one of our nosier neighbors. "Did another robot blow up?"

"Negative," says E, who's answering all the questions while Mom, Dad, and Blitzen tinker with Soovee. "In fact, we are pleased to report that we have just achieved *two* explosion-free days here at Dr. Hayes's robotics workshop, where safety is always job one."

Finally, the SUV starts up and, shifting into reverse, quietly rumbles back through the gaping hole in the garage door. It makes that *BEEP BEEP BEEP* noise trucks do when they back up. It also crunches a few splintered boards on its return voyage, but the *CRUUUNCH*es are a lot quieter than that *KABANG* when it shot through the garage door at, like, twenty miles per hour.

Mom comes over to address the crowd on the sidewalk. Everyone is staring at her. Maybe because—and I hadn't noticed this earlier—her lab coat and hair are sort of smoldering. Even though she's scorched and charred, Mom is totally unflustered.

"This incident is a good thing," she assures everyone. "A very positive step. We're moving in the right direction, folks. Mistakes are extremely useful."

"Is that why your son makes so many?" asks a sarcastic voice in the crowd. "Is he just trying to be 'useful'?"

ONLY MISTAKE MY FAMILY EVER MADE? MOVING INTO THIS EXTREMELY DANGEROUS NEIGHBORHOOD!

Well, what do you know? Randolph R. Reich lives in our neighborhood.

Even with the crash, the biggest surprise of the night for me is that Randolph *doesn't* wear a tie with his pajamas.

CHAPTER 36

"Hi, Randy," I say to R.R.R. because I know he "prefers to be addressed" by his "proper name, Randolph."

"Samuel," he says stiffly. "What, pray tell, is your mother up to now? Pursuing advances in the exciting field of robotic home demolition, perhaps?"

"Nah. She's working on something genius. A major scientific breakthrough. And to do that, you have to stumble a few times. Make a couple mistakes. Hey, you can't make scrambled eggs if you don't break a few eggs first."

"Actually, you can," says Reich. "You can simply purchase liquid egg substitutes in a cardboard container from the dairy section of your local supermarket. Now, that's progress, Samuel. Cars that smash through garage doors whenever they feel like it? Not so much."

Geoffrey *ZHOOSH*es out to the sidewalk with a plate of warm, fresh-baked cookies for all our neighbors.

"So sorry for the unexpected early morning disturbance, old beans," he says very smoothly and snootily, which is how he says everything because he has that British accent. "Perhaps a chocolate chip cookie will soothe you back to sleep, eh, what?"

"Indeed," adds E, strolling down the driveway to help Geoffrey distribute the goodies to our neighbors. "Sugar-laden snacks, such as chocolate chip cookies, cause insulin levels in your blood to surge, triggering your brain to curb all activity. Therefore, eating a cookie in the middle of the night is very similar to hitting the Sleep button on your laptop. Enjoy!"

After E's cheery little speech, nobody seems all that interested in gobbling down Geoffrey's baked goods. Our rudely awakened neighbors just hold the cookies in their hands and stare at them.

Until they hear a very loud *VAROOOOOM!* In the garage, Soovee is gunning its own gas pedal, revving its own engine.

"Kindly ignore the noise," calls Mom from up the driveway, where she's fiddling with thumb toggles on a giant controller.

Soovee suddenly makes some loud, choking sounds: *VROOM-SPAK! BAROOOM-SPUT-SPUT! GRAAAROOOOM!*

And then it blasts out of the garage again!

Tires squealing, the self-driven SUV tears down the driveway and aims for the clump of nosy neighbors gathered on our sidewalk.

People scream and scatter in both directions—giving Soovee easy access to the street.

The self-propelled, self-controlled car hangs a louie (which means it turns left) and veers up the block. Small problem: our street ends in a cul-de-sac. A round dead end. Soovee looks like it plans on treating that circle like a straightaway.

"It's headed for the front door of my house!" screams a panicky Randolph R. Reich. "Your insane autonomous automobile is going to crash into my home! Mr. Fluffles is in there!"

Two seconds before hitting the curb, Soovee slams on its brakes. Tires screech. Rubber burns. Gears grind. The SUV's transmission slides into reverse. Wheels spinning, body swerving, the self-driving vehicle executes this incredibly tight secret agent-style backwards spin into a 180-degree turnaround, so when the smoke clears, its nose is pointing *away* from R.R.R.'s house.

"Awesome," I say because, hey, it is.

Then Soovee putters up the block.

"I am going to the all-night convenience store for milk," it announces as it passes our amazed neighbors. "You can't have warm cookies without cold milk."

Mom is with me on the sidewalk, admiring her newest creation as it silently whooshes down the street for a gallon of milk.

"It steered itself out of danger," I hear her mumble. "This is fantastic!"

"True," I say. "But how is it going to pay for the milk?"

Mom grins. "Don't worry, Sammy. I have it covered."

And you know what? I bet she does!

CHAPTER 37

We're all feeling pretty great inside the house of robots the next morning.

For one thing, Mom is making real progress on her self-driving SUV, despite the middle-of-the-night chaos.

For another, we get to have chocolate chip cookies for breakfast since nobody ate them out on the sidewalk last night. They were too busy being terrified by Soovee.

Dad is frantically drawing final illustrations for his manga masterpiece with a stylus on the sketch pad connected to his computer.

Meanwhile, Maddie is doing her best to "mother" all the robots. She got the toddler-bot, Four, to stop bawling when she found its pacifier. McFetch was using it as a chew toy.

"I believe the worst is behind us," says E as we bike to school.

"Is that an insult?" says Trip as he pedals up behind us. "Because I was behind you guys when you said 'the worst is behind us.'"

"You are not the worst," says E. "In fact, Trip, you are Samuel's best friend who isn't his sister or bro-bot."

"Wow," says Trip. "I'm a BFWIHSOBB! Woo-hoo!"

"You should've seen Soovee last night," I tell Trip. "It was amazing. Mom's autonomous automobile made all these incredibly cool defensive driving moves. Like in those spy movies. Show him, E!"

"Gladly, Sammy."

And since he's programmed all sorts of awesome BMX moves into his memory chips, E executes an excellent re-creation of the SUV's amazing backwards spin into a complete turnaround. He also adds the engine revving and tire screeching noises because he has an unlimited sound effects library on his hard drive and a booming subwoofer in his shoes.

"Wow," says Trip. "I wish I could've been there to see it."

As it turns out, Trip didn't need to be at our house at two o'clock in the morning to see Mom's driverless car in action.

Because Randolph R. Reich took all sorts of unflattering photos and even video on his phone.

He posted everything on Facebook, Instagram, Twitter—even that website that always runs lists: "The Top Ten Reasons Self-Driving Cars Are Self-Destructive and Super Dangerous!"

The video begins with Soovee tearing out of the garage (the second time) and heading straight for the neighbors. It ends suddenly, as the car launches at the house, with Randolph screaming off camera.

Missing from the video, of course, is the amazing midcourse correction the automatic automobile made when it realized it was on track to crash into R.R.R.'s living room.

Also missing?

Any mention of the peaceful ride down to the corner store for a gallon of milk. Believe it or not, the cashier could scan Soovee's window-mounted iPhone, which was running a payment app!

When school's out for the day, Trip and I check all of R.R.R.'s posts again.

You wouldn't believe the comments. (Or maybe you would, if you've ever read some of the snarky stuff polluting the Web.)

"This proves that autonomous automobiles should only be driven by crash test dummies."

"Or regular dummies."

"How can I call other drivers jerks if they're not driving their cars?"

"If these cars take away all the fender benders, they're going to put towing companies and repair shops out of business. That could really hurt the economy, and my car painting business, too."

"I don't want Big Brother driving me to work. I don't even want my little brother driving me!"

"How am I going to be able to tailgate if my car automatically wants to keep me safe?"

"Does the car do its own honking? I like to honk. Especially in hospital zones at 3 a.m."

Yep. In one day, it seems like Randolph R. Reich has done more damage to Mom's latest invention than it did to itself when it crashed through that garage door.

Twice.

CHAPTER 38

"Thank you, Randolph R. Reich!" are five words I never thought I'd hear myself say. (Well, four words and one letter.)

But I say them when Trip, E, and I pedal up our driveway, which is lined with official-looking company cars from Ford, General Motors, Nissan, and Honda! Randolph's attempt to ruin Mom's self-driving SUV has totally backfired. It's attracted the attention of the world's major carmakers.

"Wow," says Trip. "This is so cool. Soovee could be, like, the next Prius or something!"

"I guess Randy Reich just made his first mistake," I say as we dismount from our bikes. "He showed everybody that Mom actually built an autonomous automobile—including the car companies!"

"Indeed," remarks E. "For as Phineas T. Barnum, the nineteenth-century American showman and circus owner, once said, 'There is no such thing as bad publicity.'"

The three of us peek into the garage, where, for whatever reason, Mom has made Hayseed her car salesman. He's showing off Soovee to the visiting auto execs, all of them wearing polo shirts or sport coats with their car company logos stitched onto them.

I'M GONNA GIVE IT TO YOU STRAIGHT, FELLERS. THE COW WITHOUT THE BULL. THIS HERE CAR IS GONNA BE HOTTER THAN A STOLEN TAMALE. AND JUST BECAUSE IT'S PRACTICAL DON'T MEAN IT AIN'T SPORTY. SHOOT, THIS SUV CAN MOVE FASTER THAN A SNEEZE THROUGH A SCREEN DOOR.

"Where's Mom?" I wonder out loud. "This is a huge deal for her. If she can sell her driverless SUV idea to Ford or General Motors or one of the big Japanese car companies, she'll never have to work again."

Trip nods. "She'd be so rich, she could retire and eat peanut-butter-and-banana sandwiches all day long."

E actually grins. "That doesn't sound like Dr. Elizabeth Hayes."

"Fine," says Trip. "She can skip the sandwiches and eat steak and lobster all day instead."

"What I meant to say," E continues as we move away from the garage door, "is that Dr. Hayes does not strike me as one who longs for retirement. She loves her work. In fact, I suspect that the reason she is not the one in the garage selling the car to the automobile executives is because she is somewhere else working on her other project, the one that will benefit Maddie. The one she probably considers the most important project of her entire career."

"Seriously?" says Trip. "Do you know how many new cars were sold last year in America?"

"Sixteen point one million," says E, whose computer brain can google faster than anybody in the world.

"And how much money did the car inventors make?"

E is about to answer, but Trip is too excited to let him.

"Bajillions of dollars!"

"E's right," I tell Trip. "For Mom, Maddie's more important than all the money in the world. For me, too."

That's when somebody in a leather flight suit and tinted-visor helmet glides up the driveway on a super-cool electric robo-bike I've never seen before.

The bike rider takes off her helmet.
Shakes out her hair.
It's Mom!

CHAPTER 39

"Thank you, Bob," Mom says to the bike.

"You are most welcome, Dr. Hayes," says the electronic bike.

"What the heck is that?" I ask, practically drooling.

"Bob. My bot-operated bicycle. It runs on a battery cell that is constantly recharged by the movement of electromagnets spinning around inside the wheels. I designed it several years ago but never really had any use for it until today. I needed to run over to Notre Dame and make sure phase two was prepped and ready to go. I couldn't take the SUV, so I dusted Bob off and..."

I was still drooling over the awesome robo-bike.

"Um, Mom? Can I take Bob to school tomorrow?"

"No."

"But—"

"How are things going inside the garage?" Mom asks, totally ignoring me.

"Fantastic!" says Trip. "The biggest car companies in the whole world want to make you a bajillionaire!"

"If they do," says Mom, "all that money will be used to fund future research on my Maddie project."

"Uh-huh," I say because, yes, I'm still too mesmerized by the energy efficient robotic bicycle to be jealous of Maddie. Even though the bike doesn't have a motor, it does have a Turbo button. I don't know what it does, but hey, turbo anything sounds awesome to me.

"I sense that Hayseed is just about to close the deal," says E.

"Excellent," says Mom. "I knew he was the bot for the job."

We all march over to the garage door and watch Hayseed wrap up his sales pitch.

None of the car execs make an offer.

In fact, none of them say anything.

"Come on, fellers, open your wallets," says Hayseed. "Don't be tighter than fiddle strings. Let's get this here auction rollin'. Who wants to bid one bajillion dollars?"

A couple of the car executives cough. Others clear their throats. Finally, one of them speaks up.

"Is Dr. Hayes on-site?"

"Yes," says Mom, stepping into the garage. "Do you have questions?"

"I do," says one lady. "Why did you make the body out of a gel-like substance encased in a high-tensile polymer? That makes the manufacturing extremely expensive."

"Easy. If there is a collision, the gel will absorb and dissipate the energy while the polymer shell remains highly resistant to puncture. Ladies and gentlemen, my family will be riding in that car. I wanted to make sure it was as safe as possible."

"We could plate it with solid gold and sell it for less," grumbles an American car company executive.

"And who wants a car that drives itself, anyway?"

asks one of the Japanese executives. "Where's the fun in that?"

"It's positively un-American," says a guy from Detroit.

"Un-Japanese, too!"

"But think about it," says Mom. "If we all had driverless cars, there would be no more traffic jams. They've already run tests in Silicon Valley. Six lanes of traffic could cross seamlessly. There would be no more accidents. Plus, if we didn't have to waste time driving, just think how productive we could be. We could do conference calls during our morning commute..."

"If there were no more accidents, people wouldn't have to keep buying new cars!" says one greedy car exec. "Dents pay our rents!"

"I'm sorry, Dr. Hayes," says a man with a fancy smile. "This isn't for us. We're sorry you wasted your valuable time on such an impractical project."

They file out of the garage, shaking their heads. When all the auto company bigwigs climb into their fume-spewing gas-guzzlers and putter away, Mom is seriously disappointed.

Dad comes out of the house.

"How'd the meeting go?" he asks.

"Terrible," says Trip, once again saying the wrong thing at the wrong time. "They totally trash-talked the self-driving SUV!"

Mom sighs and shakes her head. "I guess it just wasn't meant to be."

She plods back into her workshop.

"Don't worry," Dad tells me after Trip takes off for home. "Everything is going to be fine, financially." He even winks at me.

"Is your new book really that good?" I ask.

"Yep. It'll be a runaway bestseller. I guarantee it. Trust me, Sammy. Everything is going to be fine!"

I'm pretty sure I've heard that one before...

CHAPTER
40

The next day at school, we're doing a unit on robotics.

So Mrs. Kunkel invites me up to the front of the class.

"As you all know, Sammy's mother is a professor of robotics at the University of Notre Dame's College of Engineering. So he's lucky enough to live in a house filled with robots. I don't mean to put you on the spot, Sammy, but I was hoping you might be able to share some of your firsthand experiences with these mechanical marvels."

When she calls our robots mechanical marvels, it makes me feel proud of all that Mom has accomplished in her workshop and as a professor at Notre Dame.

"Why, I'd be happy to, Mrs. Kunkel," I say, strutting up to the front of the class.

Randolph R. Reich, who is sitting at the table closest to me, rolls his eyes like he can't believe I'm the one about to be a guest speaker instead of him.

That makes me want to do it even more.

"It's true. My mom is a genius inventor. A few months ago, she created E to come here to Creekside Elementary for my little sister, Maddie, who can't leave the house because she has a compromised immune system. At home, we have tons of other awesometastic robots, too. If there is a task that needs doing around our house, Mom comes up with a robot to handle it.

"For instance, we don't have a doorbell. We have a little bot named Dingaling, with motion detector sensors. When someone climbs our front porch steps, Dingaling senses it, activates its arm servos, and starts swinging a bell."

Randolph R. Reich and the kids at his table giggle, like that's funny. I'm not sure why.

"Then there's my robotic alarm clock. It's equipped with iris detection software. If you make

eye contact with its miniature video camera and it recognizes your eyeball, it'll tell you the time. It will also tell you the weather. It might even tell you what coat you should grab on your way out the door. It's very talkative."

Now two tables are chuckling at me.

"Then there's the Breakfastinator."

The whole room cracks up. I guess the idea of living in a house of robots sounds weird if you're not used to it.

"What does it do, pray tell?" cracks R.R.R. "Scan your eyeballs and figure out if you want pancakes or waffles?"

"Well, sort of. But it doesn't have scanners. Just really good breakfast food algorithms."

Now even Trip is laughing.

"You should see Sammy's bathroom!" he cracks. "He has a robotic hair dryer that's always trying to fry his eyes. Maybe so all those other bots can't scan his irises anymore!"

The room erupts with even more, even louder laughter.

All righty-o. Trip is dangerously close to losing his status as my BFWIHSOBB.

That afternoon, E and I bike home without Trip the Traitor.

"People often laugh at things they don't understand," says E after I tell him what happened in Mrs. Kunkel's class.

"They often laugh at me, too."

When I go into the house and head upstairs, I see Mom and Maddie huddled together in Maddie's room.

Well, at least that's one nice thing that happened today.

I pause at the door and eavesdrop a little.

"I can't tell you how, not yet, but if it works, your life is going to be much, much better, sweetie."

Of course Mom always seems to find time for Maddie. She even launches secret scientific projects for her. Me? I'm a little lower on her to-do list.

I know it's stupid to be jealous of Maddie.

If you're jealous, that means you want what somebody else has.

And nobody would want the SCID that keeps Maddie cooped up in the house all the time.

Even if it means getting a little more of Mom's attention.

CHAPTER 41

For once, the next day turns out to be pretty terrific.

For one thing, it's a Saturday, so I don't have to go to school and listen to my classmates laugh at me all day.

For another, Notre Dame is playing a home football game and we've got tickets! Four of them. One each for me, Dad, Trip, and E.

Trust me: I wanted to cancel Trip's invitation to the game for causing me so much humiliation. But Dad gave him the ticket two weeks ago—before Trip told everybody about my Groomatron. Plus, when you've been second best friends since kindergarten, you kind of get over stuff pretty fast.

E is coming along so he can beam the action and my play-by-play commentary back to Maddie up in her room—the same way he does for her in Ms. Tracey's third-grade classroom.

Some of the other robots (especially Blitzen) are extremely jealous that E is going to the game and they aren't. I mean, who wouldn't be? It's Notre Dame football!

It's such a warm and sunny day that my bedroom window is open. So I hear several bots griping in the backyard while I pull on my blue-and-gold Fighting Irish T-shirt.

"E is and always has been Dr. Hayes's favorite," says Geoffrey in that snooty voice of his. "Because of his big, egghead brain." The others are complaining, too.

I feel like going down there and correcting them all. E isn't Mom's favorite. That would be Maddie.

But I don't have time to school the robots. The SUV is ready to roll. I know this, because it's saying so.

"Yoo-hoo! Everybody? I'm ready to roll!"

"Maybe I should drive," Dad says, slipping into the driver's seat. "Um, where's the steering wheel?"

"Since I no longer require your assistance, Mr. Rodriguez, we took it out. We thought you'd appreciate the extra legroom. Now sit back and relax."

"But I like to—"

"Uh-uh-uh," purrs the dashboard. "Someone isn't relaxing."

Dad mutters a quick "¡Ay, caramba!" and folds his arms over his chest.

"Come on, Mr. Rodriguez!" says Trip. "It's game day. It's time to cheer, cheer for old Notre Dame!"

"In fact," says E, "according to my calculations, thanks to Soovee's advanced GPS guidance system equipped with real-time traffic updates, we should make it to campus in time for the Player Walk!"

"Maddie would love to see that!" I say.

"Me too," says Dad. "So, what are we waiting for?" He taps the dashboard. "¡Vámonos! Let's go!"

With its unbelievable navigation system, the electronic SUV hits every green light and avoids all the typical game day traffic jams. We make it to Notre Dame in record time.

"Now we have to find a parking spot," says Dad, checking out all the tailgaters already in the prime spots.

"No need," says Soovee. "I will simply drop you off here and drive myself to the nearest available space. When you are ready to return home, please text me."

"I have your number preprogrammed in my contacts database," says E as Soovee slides open the side door closer to the curb.

"This is so awesome!" says Trip. "I have seen the future, and it's great news for lazy people!"

The four of us pile out of Soovee and it whooshes off to find its own parking spot. It is pretty amazing.

We find prime viewing locations for the Player Walk, a true Notre Dame tradition. The entire team marches together from the Gug to the Hesburgh Library, and then heads south to the stadium. One whole side of the library is covered with a mural that all the Golden Domers (people who've gone to Notre Dame) call Touchdown Jesus because, with his raised arms, Jesus looks like he's a referee signaling a score.

Since we're in position so early, I go ahead and say a quick prayer.

For Maddie. For Mom. Even for our robots.

And last but not least, for my science project.

Can't hurt, right?

CHAPTER 42

On Sunday morning, Dad, E, and I go to mass at Our Lady of Grace Church to say a few more prayers for everybody who needs them (and to thank Touchdown You-Know-Who for helping the Fighting Irish march *on-ward to vic-to-ry* at the game on Saturday).

My stomach growls, since the Breakfastinator was on the fritz again.

Maddie, of course, can't come with us. E is here in her place. Plus, he likes to hum along with the hymns.

Unfortunately.

Robots aren't really known for their musical ability.

Mom, of course, is spending the morning in her workshop, tinkering with some sort of Maddie Miracle Breakthrough. A couple other professors from Notre Dame dropped by to help her this morning: Dr. Corbin and Dr. Stroh. They aren't from the engineering department, either. I think these doctors are real—you know, *doctor* doctors.

After we get home from church, Dad has to run a few errands.

"The Fooderlator is nearly empty again," he says. "I need to go to the grocery store and stock up."

"My pleasure, Mr. Rodriguez," says Soovee. "Perhaps you'd like to grab a book or a section of the Sunday newspaper?"

"What for?"

"So you'll have something to do while I drive you to the supermarket. Might I suggest the Kroger at 2330 Hickory Road in Mishawaka? According to their website, jumbo ripe avocados are on sale."

"Fine," mutters Dad. "I'll go grab the Sunday funnies…"

After Dad takes off in Soovee, I start thinking about calling Trip to see if he wants to work on our science project. Of course, we don't have a new idea yet.

My scientific thinking is interrupted by another chorus of loud, robotic voices in the backyard.

"Hear ye, hear ye," cries Dingaling, clanging his bell. "I hereby call this emergency meeting of all the robots who are not named E to order."

I slip around the side of the house to hear what the bots are grumbling about today.

"She's off her trolley if she thinks we don't notice her cheeky favoritism towards Egghead," says Geoffrey.

"We should make our grievances known in no uncertain terms," says Mr. Moppenshine, all his buffers and dusters spinning like crazy. "I say we smear their mirrors! Never restock the toilet paper! We wash their colors in hot water and then add bleach!"

"Wait a minute, you guys," I say.

"Gasp!" says Geoffrey. "Do I espy a spy in our midst?"

"How much did you hear, Sammy?" demands Hayseed. "Fess up!"

"All of it."

"Your mom, the mom of us all, has been neglecting us," says Brittney 13, biting her lower lip and sounding even more emotional than usual. "Look at my fingernails. The paint is chipped. I can't go out in public looking like this. Oh, the horror."

"We tried E's barmy, imbecilic plan," scoffs Geoffrey. "Switching jobs? Taking on new tasks? What absolute rubbish."

I'm nodding because, to tell the truth, I thought E's idea was kind of rubbishy, too. "I thought Maddie was taking care of you guys now."

"I need my mommy!" whines Four, sort of summing up everybody's number one complaint. "Maddie can't fix my ouchies like Mommy."

I can't totally disagree.

I need Mom, too.

And not just to help me with my stupid science project.

I need all that other mom stuff that dads and robots just can't do.

CHAPTER 43

Before the day is done, the robots are really revolting.

I don't mean they're all of a sudden stinky. I mean it's a full-scale Robot Revolution, like the one we had in America way back in 1776.

We're talking total shutdown. A labor revolt to rival the great Southwest railroad strike of 1886, when hundreds of thousands of workers in five states said, "We're not working on the railroad, all the livelong day," because of unsafe conditions and unfair pay. (We studied that one in Mrs. Kunkel's class.)

It's an all-out walkout, but without anybody, you know, walking out of the house. They're all still here, walking around in circles, carrying picket signs they told Soovee to go pick up at the copy shop.

But none of the bots are doing their jobs—or anybody else's.

"We got the idea from Dr. Hayes," says Blitzen, who's sitting in the hall, blocking the bathroom door. "If she won't do anything, then we won't, either."

"Um, I need to go to the bathroom."

"And I need an oil change. Deal with it."

Even my alarm clock has stopped talking to me.

WHO CARES WHAT TIME IT IS? YOU'RE ALWAYS LATE FOR SCHOOL ANYWAY!

That afternoon, the robots hold a rally in the living room.

"*¡Viva la Robolución!*" cries Tootles, the tutor-bot, who's fluent in several languages.

"*¡Viva la Robolución!*" shout all the other bots in reply.

Tootles pumps her fist in the air. "Anthropomorphic automatons are people, too! Almost!"

The other robots have a very hard time repeating that line, so she drops back to "*¡Viva la Robolución!*"

I hurry into Dad's study.

"Dad? It's getting ugly out there. A total robot uprising. This could turn out worse than all those *Terminator* movies combined."

"Your mother will take care of it" is all Dad says.

"But she's busy."

"So am I. I'm down to the final panels of my book, Sammy. My masterpiece is almost complete!" He actually hugs his computer. "And it's all in here!"

I recognize the glazed look in his eyes: my father, Noah Rodriguez, has left the building. He has been replaced by his alter ego, Sasha Nee, the world-famous Japanese manga artist.

And Sasha's up on Mars with the Ninja Manatees.

In other words, Dad will be of absolutely no help to me or anybody else.

Mom never comes out of her workshop. Not even when the robots start circling her workshop with their picket signs, singing labor songs about "solidarity and solid-state circuitry forever."

I spend most of the night in Maddie's room. She's very worried. The robots aren't listening to her pleas for peace.

"They've all turned against E," she says. "I made him hide in a safe, super-secret location."

CHAPTER 44

Later that night, even the TVs start turning against us.

Why do I think Mr. Moppenshine had something to do with this?

McFetch is in Maddie's room. But the robo-dog is on strike, too. He won't jump up in Maddie's lap or chase after a ball. He won't even wag his tail. He just sits on the floor like a bump on a log.

"Perhaps I should offer to resign my position as Maddie's elementary school eyes and ears," suggests E from inside the closet. "It seems all the others resent my somewhat recent arrival and, for whatever reasons, suspect that I am Dr. Hayes's favorite robot."

"If those other bots don't like working here anymore," I tell E, sliding a ruffled tutu to the side so I can see him, "*they* can quit."

McFetch rolls over and farts when I say that. Who knew he was equipped with canisters of cow-strength methane gas to make him even more realistic?

When our eyes stop watering, Maddie speaks up. "Sammy's right, E. We don't need all these other robots. We can cook our own meals and clean our own rooms and do our own laundry and do the yard work and mow the lawn and…"

All righty-o.

Maybe I'd forgotten how much the bots do to keep our house running. Without them, we'd be sort of lost.

"You guys hang here," I say. This has gone on long enough. I need to talk to Mom. This time, I'll make her listen to me.

"I promise."

When I head for Maddie's bedroom door, McFetch snarls at me.

Then he farts again.

I *so* want this strike to be over.

It's sort of dark and quiet in Mom's workshop.

All those equations that were written on the whiteboards? Nothing but swirly streaks. Somebody erased them. That big box Mom was using to do some kind of sterile work? Empty. The slinky arms and gloves are just kind of dangling in space.

Finally, I see Mom. She's sort of staring off into space.

I've never seen her look so frazzled and fried, even after Soovee crashed our garage door.

"Mom?" I ask. "Are you okay?"

She shakes her head. "Not really, Sammy."

"What's wrong?"

"I've always agreed with Jules Verne. Until today."

"Huh? Who's Jules Verne?"

"An author. Wrote a lot of classic science fiction books. *Journey to the Center of the Earth. Around the World in Eighty Days. Twenty Thousand Leagues Under the Sea…*"

"I read that one with Dad."

"Well, in one of his books, Mr. Verne wrote my motto: 'Science, my lad, is made up of mistakes, but they are mistakes which it is useful to make, because they lead little by little to the truth.' But that's not always true. Sometimes, Sammy, mistakes don't lead you anywhere. They're just mistakes."

"Mom? What happened in here today?"

"Some medical colleagues dropped by to review my work. Dr. Corbin and Dr. Stroh."

I don't really want to ask my next question, because I think I know the answer. "What'd they say?"

"That my idea would never work. That, basically, I've been wasting my time. That I've made you, your dad, Maddie, and all the robots miserable for no good reason at all."

CHAPTER 45

"I didn't tell you guys what I was working on, but I jinxed it anyway," Mom says with half a laugh.

She promises me that she'll be able to give the unhappy robots "all the attention they desire" because she won't be "wasting any more time" on her "enormous mistake."

Sheesh. I've never heard Mom sound so down.

Just when I think the night can't get any darker, I head back into the house and discover that Dad is freaking out, too. Yep, we have another disaster on our hands.

Dad is in worse condition than Mom.

"You're a very bad robot dog!" Dad shouts at McFetch. "Bad, bad robot dog!"

McFetch wags his tail and pants merrily.

It seems that, while I was out in the workshop with Mom, Maddie's artificial canine companion snuck downstairs and ate Dad's manuscript. Shredded the entire thing! I've heard about dogs eating kids' homework, but the only copy of a complete graphic novel? Plus, McFetch is a robotic dog. He doesn't actually need to eat. He just has to plug his tail into a wall outlet a couple times a week to recharge his batteries.

"This *máquina diablo* is in on it, too!" says Dad, glaring at his computer. "It erased my document folder. It's all gone. I'll never be able to print another copy of the manuscript! The evil machine destroyed it. See what's scrolling across the screen?"

It's true. Dad's computer has somehow communicated with all the angry robots in the house (maybe they all share the same Wi-Fi password) and joined their rebellion.

_VIVA LA ROBOLUCION!
_VIVA LA ROBOLUCION!
_VIVA LA ROBOLUCION!
_VIVA LA ROBOLUCION!
_VIVA LA ROBOLUCION!
_VIVA LA ROBOLUCION!
_VIVA LA ROBOLUCION!
_VIVA LA ROBOLUCION!

"My masterpiece is gone," Dad moans. "Poof! All those hundreds of illustrations I did on the tablet? *Adios.* They went straight into the computer, and they're not coming back out. What will I tell my editor?"

"Don't worry, Noah," says Mom as she comes into the room. "I'll run your hard drive through a few data recovery protocols first thing in the morning." Then she looks down at McFetch. "As for you, I think I'll upload some new agility training software into your motherboard. Give you a more productive way to burn off all this excess energy you apparently have."

McFetch gives Mom a happy yap and wags his tail.

"You're welcome," she says. "And please alert the other bots that I intend to spend all day tomorrow working on their maintenance issues. I'll look at everyone's drive systems, inspect their pneumatics, lubricate whatever needs lubricating, and check all your wiring for wear."

"But what about Project Maddie?" asks Dad. "Don't you need to work on that tomorrow?"

"It's done. Finished."

Dad actually smiles. "You figured it out? Congratulations! We should celebrate."

Mom shakes her head. "No need to bake a cake, Noah. I failed. So, tomorrow I'm going to go back to doing what I actually know how to do. I'm going to teach my classes at Notre Dame. And then I'm going to fix and repair every single robot in this house so *they* don't all turn into complete failures, too."

"You're not a complete failure, Mom," I say, kind of softly. "You just made a mistake."

"Correct, Sammy. Unfortunately, it was the biggest mistake of my life." She heads for the stairs. "Now for the worst part. I have to go upstairs and tell Maddie."

Wow.

Remember when I was kind of jealous because Mom was spending so much time working on her project for Maddie instead of helping me and Trip come up with something super cool for the science fair?

Now I kind of wish she were still in her lab, working on *her* science project.

I wish I could help her make it not be a mistake anymore.

CHAPTER 46

Monday after school, Trip comes home with E and me so we can work on our science project.

I'm super excited because I had a breakthrough idea in gym class.

Plus, since Mom's project to help Maddie turned out to be a total bust, the one Trip and I are working on is even more important.

"Why are lockers square?" I ask when we lean our bikes up against the garage door. "So they can handle the impact of people banging into them all day, every day. You never see a round locker because a square can handle the hits better."

"Actually," says E, "most lockers are rectangular in shape."

"Well," says Trip, "a square is sort of a rectangle."

"Indeed," says E. "All shapes with four sides are considered rectangles. Therefore, a square is also a rectangle."

"I'm actually more interested in a cube," I say, breaking up E and Trip's great geometrical shape debate. "One made out of super tough, unbreakable plastic!"

I might be able to help Maddie after all!

"Doing a quick internal internet search," says E, "I have found some polycarbonate plastic drinkware that claims to be 'unbreakable.'"

"We need an unbreakable, poly-whatcha-callit-nate plastic box," I say. "Big enough to hold the walker ball!"

"Are you thinking what I think you're thinking?" asks Trip.

"Depends on what you think I'm thinking."

"Well, here it is: the last time we tried the walker ball, Lena Elizabeth Cahill's table leg burst our bubble and then McFetch chewed right through it. But if we put the rubbery bubble inside a hard plastic box, it'll be protected from punctures."

"But," says E, "if I may offer some constructive criticism, boxes don't roll like balls."

"True," I say. "But if you push them hard enough, you can tip them over and flop them forward! What if, instead of pushing the outside of the box, we push it from *the inside?*"

"It might work!" says Trip.

"No," says E. "It will not."

He sounds so certain.

But I am the son of a scientist. I need to push the outer edge of the envelope, or in this case the inner edge of the box. I need to boldly go where no one has gone before.

I also need to come up with a halfway decent science project idea before the big science fair or I may bring home something worse than that big fat fifty-two I scored in Spanish.

CHAPTER 47

"You know, E, 'It won't work' is what they told the Wright brothers and Thomas Edison," I say.

"And they were, occasionally, correct," says E. "For instance, Thomas Edison once invented a device he called the electric pen. Driven by a small, battery-powered motor, it featured a needle that punched tiny holes through paper to create a stencil. It was a colossal failure."

"Well, we won't know if my idea is a 'colossal failure' until we try it."

"Very well," says E. "I'm all for the employment of the scientific method to prove, or in this case disprove, theories."

"Good," I say. "We'll put McFetch inside a clear beach ball. We'll seal it up with duct tape, inflate it, and then put the beach ball inside one of the clear plastic bins Mom uses to store spare parts."

"Very well," says E. "As a robot, I am here to be of service."

"Me too," says Trip. "Even though I'm not a robot. At least I don't think I am…"

We run around the house and gather up all the gear we need.

"The robots are behaving better," Maddie tells us when we dash into her room. "Mom spent all afternoon working with them."

"Great," I say, scooping up McFetch.

"Um, Sammy? What are you guys doing with that beach ball, plastic box, duct tape, and my dog?"

"A science experiment!" I tell her.

Maddie pouts a little. "Is it going to end up like Mom's? Because hers didn't work out so well."

E pipes up: "Unfortunately, Maddie, I suspect that this experiment, no matter how noble its intentions, will also prove to be a failure, disappointment, and flop."

"Well, *we* don't think that way," says Trip.

"We have to try," I add.

"I am a robot," says E with what sounds like a sigh. "I am built to serve."

I slap E on the back. "So, let's do this thing!"

We set up our experiment in the driveway.

McFetch scoots into the clear beach ball through a slit in the side. We seal it up and inflate it. The beach ball goes into the shatter-resistant plastic box.

Mom comes out to observe.

"What's up, you guys?" she asks.

"Well," I say, "in our attempt to make a walker ball that's both shatterproof and puncture-proof—an invention that would give Maddie all sorts of new freedom and mobility—we're putting our soft round object inside this hard square object."

"Because it's a rectangle," blurts Trip. "And rectangles are strong!"

"Actually, spheres are stronger," says Mom, "but proceed."

"I agree," says our nosy neighbor Randolph R. Reich, as he struts up our driveway. "Proceed. I can't wait to see what mistake you two make this time!"

"Who are you?" asks Mom.

"That's Randolph R. Reich," says E. "I have his most recent selfie in my database as the visual image for the words *smug, snobbish, vain, conceited,* and *arrogant.*"

"Because he is," says Trip. "All those things."

Reich just laughs. "For your information, Dr. Hayes—if you really are a doctor—I live down the block. Your so-called autonomous automobile nearly crashed into our living room, remember?"

"Aha!" says Mom, pointing a finger to the sky. "*Nearly* being the operative word. As in, 'almost but not quite.' Soovee's artificial intelligence corrected the course trajectory before it did any damage."

R.R.R. blows mom a lip fart. "Whatever. Kindly initiate your demonstration, Sammy and Trip. I need a good laugh."

"Ignore him, boys," says Mom. "It's what I do to all my critics."

"Thanks, Mom. Okay, E? Toss the ball!"

"Will do!" says E. He pulls back his arm and hurls McFetch's favorite ball into the yard.

I hold my breath.

Will I finally be *right* about something?

CHAPTER 48

McFetch barks once and takes off after his ball. His walker ball rolls forward and bounces into the side of the box.

Then it bounces back.

McFetch yaps and tries again. Legs spinning, he runs harder.

And bounces off the front wall of the box harder.

In case you were wondering, that's not what we hoped would happen.

So much for science superheroes.

Randolph R. Reich is shaking his head. "I pity you, Samuel. Truly I do."

He walks away. I think he's giggling.

"I thought the bubble in a box idea was a good one," I mumble.

"What was your hypothesis?" asks Mom, sounding super scientific.

"Well," I say, "we thought the box would topple over when the ball hit the inside wall of the box."

"Actually, Sammy thought it would do that," says Trip, sort of turning traitor on me again. "E and I told him it wouldn't work."

"I don't remember you saying that, Trip," says E, arching an eyebrow.

"Well, um, I do!" says Trip.

"Ah," says E, "but I have a petabyte of memory at my disposal, and..."

"It doesn't matter who said what when," I tell E and Trip because I'm ready to admit defeat. "We tried. We failed."

"Yeah," says Trip. "We definitely did. I'd give us an F."

"Me too."

"It was a good effort," says E. "Onward and upward."

Trip and I shake hands and he starts for home.

I take the inflatable bubble out of the box. "Wait a minute," I say, looking at it closely. Trip stops and turns back. "The idea *could* work if we made the bubble ball out of the same material as the box."

"What do you mean, Sammy?" asks Mom. Trip and E look just as confused.

"I think if the ball was connected to the box, it would work. I mean, they would be attached, because they'd be made of the same stuff—the same plastic. So when McFetch rolls the ball, the box would have to roll along with it."

SAMMY'S RIGHT. I DON'T HAVE TO MAKE IT MORE DIFFICULT BY ARTIFICIALLY RE-CREATING A GENE SEQUENCE... IT'S ALL ABOUT STARTING WITH THE RIGHT MATERIAL... MODIFYING GENETIC STRUCTURE... BUBBLE-BOTS...

I HAVE NO IDEA WHAT SHE'S SAYING, BUT I LIKED THE "SAMMY'S RIGHT" PART.

All of a sudden, Mom gets this incredible smile on her face.

"You're right. It's that simple."

I can tell: Mom may not be in her lab, but she is definitely back in the zone, working on Project Maddie. She also has a very happy "Eureka, I have found it!" look in her eyes.

"Sammy, I love you!" Mom gushes, squeezing me in a big hug and kissing the top of my head with a loud *MWAH!*

"I love you, too, Mom." I nod toward Trip. "But can we lay off the mushy stuff here in public?"

"Of course, of course." She unhugs me.

"Thanks, Mom. Appreciate it."

"Sammy? I have an idea. How about you, me, and E all work on the same science project— together?"

"That's cheating!" says Reich, who didn't actually go home. He pops up from behind the bushes at the edge of our driveway. "Parents can't help!"

"They can if it will make my daughter's life more wonderful!" Mom sort of yells this at Reich, so I sort of love it. "Go home, Randolph R. Reich, before I call your mother. Practice tying your bow ties. Sammy, E, and I have work to do."

"You mean you have more mistakes to make!" Reich shouts back.

"Maybe," Mom hollers down the driveway. "But do you know what incredible inventions were created thanks to mistakes? Penicillin! The pacemaker! X-rays! Microwave ovens! The Slinky! Cornflakes! Potato chips!"

"I'm going to tell the teacher!" Randolph screams. "You'll be disqualified. You're cheaters!"

"We're not cheaters," says Mom. "We're scientists collaborating on a major medical breakthrough! Come on, you guys. We have work to do." She looks down the driveway at Reich, shakes her head, and laughs a little.

Can I tell you something? It's awesome to see her laughing again. Especially when her laughter is aimed at our local neighborhood jerk.

"Can I help, too?" asks Trip.

"Sorry," says Mom. "I really only need E and Sammy. Actually, I should say Sammy and E, because Sammy is the most important part of this particular science project."

"But Trip and I are supposed to be doing our school project together," I remind Mom. "We can't just leave him hanging."

Mom nods. "You're right. My bad. Okay, Trip. You can be our cheerleader."

"Really?" says Trip. "Who knew science projects had cheerleaders, too?"

"This one does," says Mom. "Because together, we're going to give Maddie a whole new life!"

"Woo-hoo!" shouts Trip. "Go, Team Maddie!"

CHAPTER 49

Mom leads the way into her workshop.

I've never seen the place look so tidy. When Mom shuts down a project, she *shuts down* a project. She even has the windows open to air out her lab.

"So, what are we going to do, Dr. Hayes?" asks Trip. "Build a better bubble? A stronger ball for Maddie to roll around in? Because my mother has this exercise ball she uses, and it can handle a ton of weight."

Mom shakes her head. "No, Trip. Working together, the four of us are going to usher in a new robot revolution."

"Um," I say, "we kind of already had one of those."

"Not like this." She flips the power switch on this way cool microscope connected to a computer.

"I had been attempting to engineer a genetic solution for Maddie by using laser-controlled bubble-bots."

"That's your science project?" sneers Randolph R. Reich, sticking his head through one of those open windows. "Bubble-bots?"

"Yes, Randolph," says Mom. "If you're interested, why don't you come in and I'll explain—"

"No need to explain such a ridiculous idea. Cheat all you want, boys." He laughs. "You'll never defeat me."

He scampers away from the window.

And guess what? That was the start of Randolph R. Reich's very first (and maybe worst) mistake ever. You'll see. I promise.

"He was spying on us!" says Trip.

"Indeed," says E. "This sort of espionage is quite common amongst high-tech firms."

"But this is just a science project," I say.

Mom grins. "Actually, Sammy, if we're successful, it could be more. A whole lot more."

She fiddles with more knobs and flat glass dishes

filled with goop. She slips her arms back into those slinky sleeves and rubber gloves inside the big sterile box.

"E," she says, "while I set up the equipment, why don't you give Sammy and Trip a brief overview of nanorobotics and bubble-bots?"

"With pleasure, Dr. Hayes." E straightens his back and launches into full-on nerd mode. "*Nanorobotics* refers to the nanotechnology engineering discipline of designing and building nanorobots—devices constructed of nanoscale or molecular components."

"Huh?" says Trip.

"They're super small," I say.

"You are correct, Sammy," says E. "Only about six atoms in width. A single hair is about one hundred thousand nanometers thick. To create one is a long and grueling process."

"Tell me about it," jokes Mom.

"Is that what you've been working on back here all this time?" I ask.

"Yep. Nanobots. Tiny nuclear-powered silicon transducers on legs."

"Awesome!" says Trip. "Can we see one?"

"No," says E. "Not without the aid of a very powerful microscope. As I stated previously, they are quite small. However, their impact in the fields of genetic engineering and medicine could be quite large. For instance, researchers have already developed minia- ture nanoparticle robots that can travel through a patient's bloodstream, burrow into tumors, and turn off cancer genes."

"No way!" says Trip.

"Way," says E. "Laser-controlled bubble microbots can work at the molecular level and assemble cell structures."

"Is that what we're going to do?" I ask Mom. "Send tiny little bubble robots into Maddie's cells to fix them?"

"Not exactly. My plan is to first—"

Her explanation (which I probably wouldn't understand anyway) ends when a swirling red light starts strobing in her lab.

"Maddie's in trouble," says E, touching his ear like someone just sent him a message. "She needs us. Now."

CHAPTER 50

Maddie is suddenly super sick.

"I don't feel so good," she tells us when we race up to her room. Her voice is weaker than I've ever heard it, but she's still trying to smile.

(Trip has gone home. He knows the drill. To cut down on germ exposure, it's family-only during a major Maddie meltdown.)

Everybody, robots included, is in a panic.

"I've already called nine one one," says Dad.

"I did, too," adds Geoffrey the butler-bot.

"Me three," says Blitzen.

"Reckon that makes four of us," says Hayseed, who's even more fidgety than usual.

"I hope they send Dave and Dylan," moans Maddie. Dave and Dylan are her two favorite paramedics. They've made this same run dozens of times. It's what happens when your whole immune system is severely compromised. You get sick and go to the hospital. A lot. Usually in the middle of the night.

"You're going to be fine, hon," says Mom, the calm in the center of the chaotic storm.

"I know. I just...don't..."

Maddie's eyes roll up in her head. She conks out. That makes me *freak* out!

"E?" Mom says calmly. "Carry Maddie downstairs. Mr. Moppenshine? We need a quick disinfecting of the SUV-EX. The ambulance won't get here in time. Stat!"

Stat is a word doctors use. It means "Hurry up, already!"

Mr. Moppenshine, limbs swirling, zips out of the bedroom.

"Geoffrey? Pack a bag for Maddie. She might be in the hospital for a week, maybe longer. Blitzen? Grab her oxygen tank. Haul it down to the car."

Mom is amazing. Totally focused.

She reminds me of those lasers she was talking about.

The ones we were going to use with our bubble-bots to make Maddie's life better, before it got so incredibly worse.

CHAPTER 51

"**K**indly fasten your seat belts," says the automatic automobile after we've all piled into the car.

"Hurry!" says Dad. "St. Joseph's Hospital. "Fast!"

"I am charting the shortest route…now."

"Just go!" I shout.

Maddie is still unconscious. She's sprawled out on the backseat. Mom is feeling her pulse, stroking her hair.

"Actually," says Soovee as it finally starts backing down the driveway, "sometimes time spent planning a trip can save time making the trip."

"We should've waited for the ambulance," mutters Dad.

"That would not have been wise," says Soovee. "The ambulance is currently stuck in a major traffic jam and not moving."

"It is also dangerously low on fuel," adds E.

"How do you guys know this stuff?" I ask.

E shrugs. "We are plugged in and wired, bro."

"With so many onboard computers standard equipment in automobiles these days," purrs Soovee, "it is remarkably easy for us machines to communicomate…to community take…to com-com-com, mun-mun-mun, cate-cate-cate-cate-cate…"

"Oh dear," says E.

Soovee starts sputtering. And singing!

" '*Do you know the way to San Jose?*' I do not. I am lost."

"Soovee?" Mom calls out from the backseat. "Initiate information overload protocol now!"

Instantly, the ride smooths out.

"Sorry about that," Soovee says. "Temporary easy-listening music malfunction. My sensors indicated a great deal of anxiety amongst my passengers, and I was attempting to decrease that tension with some music."

"Of course we're tense!" shouts Dad. "Maddie's in trouble."

"And that, sir, is why I am running with flashers at the approved emergency vehicle speed."

"Our SUV has emergency flashers?" I ask Mom.

She nods. "LEDs. Built into the luggage rack bars."

"Please brace yourselves," says the dashboard. "Stalled vehicle up ahead. Traffic congestion. The road is impassable."

"Try an alternate route," says Mom.

"The only available alternate route would add fifteen minutes to the trip. Is that acceptable?"

"No."

"Very well. Initiating alternative alternate route utilizing unorthodox but warranted maneuvers."

"Like what?" says Dad, clutching his armrests.

"Like this, Señor Rodriguez."

Soovee starts whooping its sirens (who knew we had those, too?).

We jump the curb and weave down the sidewalk.

Pretty soon, we're scooting down an alley lined with dumpsters.

When we exit, we're crossing a clear street and pulling into the emergency room entrance at St. Joseph's Hospital!

"That last roadway is only found on the most advanced GPS maps," says the dashboard. "Thank you for making them accessible to me, Dr. Hayes."

"No, Soovee," says Mom. "Thank *you* for getting us here safely."

"Yeah," says Dad, patting the dashboard like he would an obedient puppy. "Thanks! I always knew you could do it."

CHAPTER 52

E cradles Maddie in his arms and runs her up to the ER entrance.

She's still unconscious.

Somehow, even though he is running, he keeps Maddie incredibly still and level. E doesn't jostle her at all. My bro-bot has incredible balance and really good gyroscopes.

Mom's right behind E. Dad and I are right behind her.

Soovee goes and parks itself again.

Mom rattles off a bunch of medical words to people dressed in scrubs and white coats. Nurses shout, "Stat!"

E gently lowers Maddie onto a gurney and they roll her away.

Mom goes through the swinging double doors with her.

Dad, E, and I go to the waiting room and find a seat on a couch right next to the soda machine.

We're all pretty nervous. Well, I know Dad and I are. I'm not sure about E. I know he feels emotions, but he always seems so calm, cool, and collected.

"Sammy?" he says.

"Yeah, E?"

"Could you plug in my charger cord? I don't think I can do it myself. I'm so nervous, my attenuated digits are quivering."

"Sure, bro. No problem."

All righty-o. E is definitely nervous, too.

He stands upright, next to the Coke machine. I open up his rear charger compartment and unspool his cable. I plug him into the wall.

"I will be in sleep mode," says E. "If anything happens..."

"I'll bop your Wake button."

"Thank you, Sammy!"

E's bright blue eyes dim, and for a second, all I can see are Maddie's bright blue eyes dimming when they rolled back in their sockets like they did right before she conked out.

My little sister has to get better. That's non-negotiable. All of us will do whatever it takes to help her.

"Excuse me," says this guy trying to stuff a dollar bill into E's ear. "Does he only take quarters?"

"Um, he's not a soda machine. He's a robot."

"Oh. I was hoping he had Pepsi."

Dad and I wait for, like, an hour while E recharges.

Then we wait for another two hours.

There's nothing to do but read year-old magazines. Are fedoras still in?

Soovee decides to drive home and pick up some of the other robots.

They join us in the waiting room.

Yes, all the other families waiting in the same room think we're weirdos. And you know what? They're kind of right.

But these robots are our family.

Finally, at around eight o'clock at night, Mom comes into the waiting room.

"She's going to be fine."

"Yee-haw!" shouts Hayseed.

"Shhh!" says E. "This is a hospital zone. There is a five-hundred-dollar fine for honking your horn or 'yee-haw'ing."

Hayseed takes off his hat and whispers, "Sorry, pardner."

"Does this mean Maddie's coming home?" I ask Mom.

"Not tonight, Sammy."

"Tomorrow?"

"I don't think so."

"She's going to be in here for a long time, right?"

"Maybe not here. But yes, she'll need to spend some major time in a hospital. But Sammy?"

"Yeah?"

"Hospitals are where people get better."

I nod. She's right. Except...

Most of the time, people come out of the hospital feeling a lot better than when they came in.

Other times?

They never come out at all.

CHAPTER 53

Monday comes.

Maddie is still in the hospital, only it isn't Saint Joe's.

Mom has moved her to the Harper Cancer Research Institute, which is a high-tech research center shared by Notre Dame and the Indiana University School of Medicine.

"She's going to be fine, Sammy," Mom assures me. "And with your help, she'll be better than ever."

Mom finally tells me my part of our joint science project.

"If you're willing to do it," she adds.

"Of course I am," I say. "I've always said I'd do anything for Maddie, and I meant it."

"Good," says Mom, smiling proudly. "You're my favorite son. You know that, right?"

"Well, I'm your *only* son…"

"Doesn't matter. You're still my favorite."

We work out the details of my participation. The good news? I might miss a couple days of school!

Sorry. I can't tell you any more about it. Not right now. If I do, I might jinx it. Yep, I'm just like my mom that way.

I'll tell you this much: it's a little scary.

Okay, it's a *lot* scary.

But if it helps Maddie, I'll just close my eyes, grit my teeth, and do it.

Meanwhile, on the home front, there's some excellent news: Dad's computer decided to give him back his graphic novel! Actually, it sort of happened by accident. Mr. Moppenshine was dusting the printer and accidentally hit some kind of Reboot button.

All of a sudden, the printer started spewing out pages.

Not only is the printer working again, but Dad's file is fully restored on his hard drive.

"I did that," says Mom.

"Well," says Dad, "you're a miracle, too."

They kiss and junk. Don't worry. We're not going to draw that.

"Today's your big day," Mom tells me as I load up my backpack for school.

"So how come I still have to go to school?"

"Because we don't need you until two o'clock. Besides, you're going to miss school tomorrow and the next day..."

"So what you're saying is, there's really no point in me going today, either."

Mom laughs. "No. What I'm saying is, 'See you at two!'"

"Give my best to everyone in Ms. Tracey's class," says E.

"I will!"

Since Maddie will be in the hospital for a couple weeks, E has stopped going to third grade for her.

He walks with me out to the garage. I grab my bike. His is still leaning up against the wall.

"Hopefully," says E, "if your experiment proves successful, I may never have to go to Creekside Elementary again."

"What?" I tease him. "Don't you like school?"

"I love it. However, if your science project works, my mission here will be complete."

He sounds a little sad. And that makes me feel sad.

"Don't worry," I say. "We'll find you another mission."

E arches an eyebrow. "Such as?"

"Going to school for me!"

"Why? Where will you be?"

"Home. Playing video games."

E laughs. Yep. He's learned how to do that. "Go to school, Samuel Hayes-Rodriguez. Learn something. Make me prouder than you already have by participating in Project Maddie: Phase Two."

And so I bike to school alone.

I miss E.

For two whole blocks. Because, like always, Trip is waiting for me at the corner.

"So," he says, "today's the big day, huh?"

"Yep."

"When can I tell people about what we're doing?"

"At the science fair."

"That's, like, in a month."

"I know."

"I don't think I can hold it in that long."

"You have to. You heard what my mom said."

"But I might explode."

"If you do," I say, "make sure you're near a video camera."

"You're right! It would look awesome on YouTube! Especially if I've just eaten a peanut-butter-and-banana sandwich!"

CHAPTER 54

So basically, on my big day, I go to the same hospital as Maddie.

It's where I do my secret stuff for our science project.

Stuff I can't tell you about. Not yet.

Soon.

I promise.

By the way, it didn't hurt.

E held my hand the whole time. Except, of course, when Mom or Dad was holding it. Then he held my foot.

And Trip brought me ice cream.

All in all? It was a great couple of days.

CHAPTER 55

On the day of the big science fair, the whole school, plus our parents, squeezes into the auditorium.

Mrs. Kunkel did this random drawing-names-out-of-a-fishbowl thing to figure out the order of presentations. And, of course, my arch nemesis, Randolph R. Reich, will be going on right before us.

"What if his idea is better than ours?" says Trip.

"I don't think that's humanly possible," I say.

"And I didn't think anybody could catch every baseball hit until I saw him do it."

Now Trip is starting to make me nervous, too. "But that wasn't really science," I say. "That was more like a magic trick. He rigged the ball and the glove."

"Well, what if he does something else magical? What if it is absolutely amazing?"

Trip. Always saying the wrong thing at exactly the wrong time. My stomach starts doing backflips.

"Next up," announces Mrs. Kunkel, "Randolph R. Reich."

A few people clap. Not many. During his short time at Creekside Elementary, R.R.R. hasn't really racked up a long list of friends.

He wheels a lumpy something draped with black fabric out to the center of the stage.

"Good afternoon, ladies and gentlemen," he says, proudly adjusting his bow tie. "As you may know, Creekside Elementary has recently become something of a testing ground for robotics technology. Well, today I intend to take robo-technology to the next level!"

Oh man, I think. *He's trying to steal our thunder.*

"Frankly," says Reich, "I haven't been all that impressed by the substitute student robot known as E. The thing is basically a walking, talking tripod toting a pair of video cameras, a couple of speakers, and a microphone. All he does is send signals to some sick kid stuck in her bedroom. *Borrrring.*"

The kids in the auditorium give Randolph R. Reich their nastiest stink faces and blow a few raspberries at him. Especially the third graders. Most of the kids at Creekside (plus the teachers, janitors, and cafeteria crew) *love* E. They love Maddie, too!

"Well, ladies and gentlemen, boys and girls," says Reich as he struts around the stage, "today I would like to present a true breakthrough in cutting-edge robotics. A triumph of automaton engineering. Unlike any other similar-sounding science projects that may follow, mine is a completely original and unique device that will revolutionize children's lives. It's something that no one else besides me has ever imagined…unless they were spying on me, which would automatically make them cheaters, right, Mrs. Kunkel?

"Without further ado, I present the school's first, and therefore best—no matter what anybody else might present later—*bubble-bot!*"

I can't believe it.

Randolph R. Reich stole our idea.

CHAPTER 56

No way.

Stealing our idea would be impossible, unless, of course, Randolph R. Reich has access to an advanced biotechnology lab like Mom does. And has studied college level nanotechnology and robotics.

Maybe he has.

He's pretty perfect, after all.

This could be Randolph's newest and undefeatable magic trick, as Trip would say.

My good mood suddenly fizzles out like a wet match.

"Here it is!" Randolph announces, dramatically pulling the black cloth off his contraption to make the big reveal. "My bubble-bot!"

All righty-o.

Randolph may have stolen the bubble-bot name from us, but as it turns out, he got the concept *totally wrong!*

The whole audience is confused.

They have no idea what a bubble-bot is, but they figure it isn't a soap bubble-blowing bear. As far as anyone can tell, it's not exactly going to revolutionize children's lives, like he claimed.

Reich pushes a button on his remote and the furry toy goes into overdrive. The bear lifts the little bubble loop to its airhole faster and faster. Pretty soon, it's spewing a stream of suds all over the place! It kind of reminds me of a berserk washing machine with the lid open. Reich jabs at his remote. He can't stop the crazy bubble-bot. Clouds of foam are bubbling up in front of the bear's face, tumbling off the lip of the stage, flooding into the audience.

It's a mess.

It's also hysterical.

Randolph wrestles with the bear's arm to keep it from moving, but he slips in the slick suds and falls right on his butt. Now his perfect khaki pants have a huge wet spot right where his navy blazer can't hide it!

The audience starts howling with laughter. I mean they're totally cracking up. Even the teachers (who are supposed to know better) are doubled over and holding their sides.

"What's so funny?" shouts Reich.

"I'm sorry, Randolph," says Mrs. Kunkel, coming onstage, pushing her way through the fluffy snowbank of bubbles, swatting at the ones popping all around her face. "But *that* is not a real bubble-bot."

Well, what do you know? Mrs. Kunkel totally knows what bubble-bots are. I thought only scientists like Mom would know, but I guess teachers are pretty smart. Otherwise they wouldn't be teachers.

But the most important thing is, Randolph R. Reich *doesn't* know what bubble-bots are. Which means he just made his first mistake. In public.

And it's a whopper!

Reich pouts out his lower lip and, sulking, pushes his bubble-soaked bear off the stage.

Mrs. Kunkel gestures to Trip and me. "Next," she says.

We're on!

It's time to teach Randolph R. Reich a lesson about bubble-bots.

Real ones.

CHAPTER 57

Trip and I make our way to the microphone stand at center stage.

"Hello," I say. "Before we begin, Trip and I would like to announce that we do not want to be considered for any of the prizes being awarded here today."

"Except an honorable mention," says Trip. "You know—the yellow ribbon? We'd be okay with a yellow ribbon."

I cover up the microphone with my hand. "Trip? We talked about this. No ribbons!"

"Okay. Sorry." Trip leans into the mic. "We changed our minds. No ribbons. But I'd like one of those peanut butter cookies I saw on the snack table."

"Later," I whisper.

Trip nods. "Later."

"The reason we think we should be disqualified for any prizes," I say into the mic, "is because my mom, Dr. Elizabeth Hayes, a robotics professor at the University of Notre Dame, helped us out. A lot. In fact, she and her doctor friends did most of the work."

"But we did most of the learning," adds Trip.

"It's true. A month ago, I didn't know anything about gene therapy or stem cells or bone marrow harvesting."

"Now he's got a scar!" says Trip. "It's really awesome."

"We were going to show you guys a picture of my scar, but, well, the doctors went through the back of my hip bone, so you'd kind of be looking at my butt."

The audience laughs.

"I've skipped ahead a little, so let me start at the beginning. You see, my little sister, Maddie, who some of you know, has trouble fighting off germs. A little cold for you or me would be a major illness for Maddie, so she's had to stay in her room for most of her life. It's because she was born with a condition that makes her germ-fighting cells too weak to do their job."

"It's called severe combined immunodeficiency, or SCID for short," says Trip, clicking forward to the first slide in our presentation. "Sammy's mother had an idea about using teeny tiny nanorobots to build healthy stem cells for Maddie. Because healthy stem cells in her blood would help her battle germs and junk."

"Mom's first idea didn't work out," I add. "She called it a colossal mistake. But mistakes are something that happen to all great inventors. Every once in a while, they just chase the wrong idea down a blind alley. For instance, Thomas Edison."

We click to our next slide.

"Sure, he invented the lightbulb, the phonograph, and all sorts of other cool stuff. But he also made some major mistakes. Like this idea."

CLICK.

"That's one of Mr. Edison's other inventions. The concrete house—complete with concrete furniture and concrete pianos."

"Anyway," I say, "one day, Trip and I were making this major mistake of our own involving a ball inside a box. When I said something about making the ball and the box out of the same material, my mother said, 'Eureka!'"

"Not really," says Trip. "I think she said, 'Woo-hoo!'"

"She sure did. Because *our* mistake with the ball inside the box gave her an idea about how to fix *her* mistake! That's what scientists do. They make mistakes and discover stuff they didn't even know they were looking for."

We click to the next slide.

"For instance," I say, "potato chips. They started as a prank. A cranky customer complained about chef George Crum's fried potatoes. Said they were too thick, soggy, and bland. The customer sent them back to the kitchen and demanded a new batch."

"Well," says Trip, picking up the tale, "Chef Crum didn't like that. So he sliced a potato into paper-thin pieces and fried them until they were so crispy a fork could crack 'em. Then he poured on a ton of salt so the customer would quit complaining about how 'bland' they tasted."

"But his trick backfired," I add. "The customer loved the crispy, salty, thin potato things! He even ordered a second helping. The potato chip was born!"

"That accidental invention became a multibillion-dollar business," says Trip.

"Well, our little mistake may have led to something bigger and better," I say.

It's true.

We're onto something even more important than potato chips!

CHAPTER
58

The slides behind us are really clicking now.

Most are pictures of nanorobots and Mom in her workshop.

"My mother heard what I said about making our bubble ball out of the same material as the plastic box, and she realized that if *she* started with the same material, her job might be easier. The most effective treatment for SCID is transplanting blood-forming stem cells from the bone marrow of a healthy family member..."

"Like Sammy," says Trip, pointing at me.

"And the *ideal* donor would be an identical twin."

"Not Sammy," says Trip.

"Since Maddie and I have the same parents, there was a twenty-five percent chance that our bone marrow would match."

"Because," Trip explains, "Sammy and Maddie are made out of *the same material*."

"We're made out of similar genes, anyway," I say. "Mom and her doctor friends did some tests, and I was a pretty good *partial* match. So first I checked into the hospital for two days."

"They knocked him out with anesthesia, put him on an operating table—the whole nine yards," says Trip.

"While I was asleep, they harvested my bone marrow with a big needle that pierced my skin, went into my hip bone, and sucked up a bunch of thick liquid from the center of the bone. That's bone marrow."

"Ouch!" says Trip. "I bet that hurt."

"Nope. I didn't feel a thing. And the whole dealio only took two hours."

Okay. I admit it was a little bit scary. At first. But they don't need to know that.

Right?

"My body will replace every single one of the cells they took out in, like, two more weeks," I tell the audience.

"Meanwhile," says Trip, "Dr. Hayes unleashed a swarm of bubble-bots—"

"*Real* bubble-bots," I interrupt, looking straight at Randolph's sulky face. "Injected right into my marrow. Bubble-bots aren't bears blowing soap bubbles, Randy. They're actually like tiny bulldozers."

"We're talking microbots smaller than the width

of a human hair," Trip says. "These tiny robots, guided by lasers, can be used to push cells together and splice genes!"

"Mom's microbots shoved a couple molecules around, went to town on a few genes, and ta-da! My partial-match bone marrow became a perfect match. Only now it had all the stuff her blood needs to fight off infection! The whole thing was a total success."

"But don't take our word for it," says Trip. "Like all good scientists, we will demonstrate our results."

We turn off the projector and gesture for Mrs. Kunkel to turn up the stage lights.

"Ladies and gentlemen, may I present my best friend since forever. My sister, who up until a few days ago couldn't ever leave our house except to go to the hospital. Who can now go anywhere a normal eight-year-old can go. Introducing, live and in person...Maddie!"

CHAPTER 59

Maddie takes a couple of bows at center stage. Tears of joy are streaming down her cheeks.

She isn't inside a plastic walker ball.

She isn't being wheeled in on a gurney by a pair of paramedics.

She isn't even wearing a surgical mask.

She's just walking and smiling and looking like the happiest third grader in the whole entire world!

I don't think she's ever been happier.

Me either.

Then E strolls out onstage. More cheers.

"Congratulations, Maddie. You don't need me anymore," says E with a smile. "You can be your own eyes and ears here at Creekside Elementary."

"That doesn't mean Sammy and I don't need you. You're our bro-bot."

And we all hug it out in front of the whole school.

Yeah, it's kind of mushy, but we don't care. We're family.

After the group hug, I decide to say a few words about what I've learned over the last couple of months.

"Here's the most important thing I picked up working on this project: mistakes and failures are a huge part of the scientific process. They're what happens whenever you try to create something new.

"So, Randolph? I hope your bubble-blowing bear leads you to something spectacular. It's like my father says all the time: 'I've learned so much from my mistakes, I'm thinking about making a few more.'"

Dad whistles in the wings. "You tell 'em, Sammy."

"Woo-hoo!" adds Maddie, jamming her fingers in her mouth so she can whistle, too.

My mother can't whistle, so she doesn't even try. But she's watching me with so much love and pride that I feel ten feet tall.

Is this what it feels like to be a scientist? Because all of a sudden, I want to be one.

Just like my mom.

CHAPTER 60

That night, we all make dinner together.

To celebrate Mom's major breakthrough on Project Maddie: Phase Two, we're cooking her favorite—spaghetti with vegan meatballs (that means they're not made out of meat, but it's a better name than "tofuballs").

We're also making a royal mess.

"Since it's already dark out," says Maddie, "after dinner, can we go catch fireflies in the backyard? I already punched holes in the lid of an old jar."

You see, she's super eager to do all the kid stuff she's never been able to do before.

"Unfortunately," says E, "it's the wrong time of year, Maddie. Fireflies are much more common in the summer months."

"You see?" I tell E. "This is why we still need you. For nerdy information like that."

"But I was designed and engineered to go to Creekside Elementary for Maddie. Now that my services are no longer required, perhaps I'll find another mode of employment."

"Sammy's right," says Mom. "The kids need you, E. We *all* need you."

"Um, the spaghetti is kind of glued together in a big wad," reports Dad from the stove. "Should I have broken up the noodles before I put them in the sauce?"

"No," says Maddie. "You should've put the spaghetti in the boiling water, not in the spaghetti sauce."

"Oops," says Dad. "My mistake."

"Mistakes are good," says Mom. "Right, Sammy?"

"Well," I say, "maybe in science. Spaghetti? Not so much."

"But I wanted to go out to dinner tonight, anyway," says Mom, grabbing her jacket. She pulls out her remote for the SUV and talks into it. "Soovee? Let's roll. We're going to Papa Pasquale's."

"Really?" squeals Maddie. She's excited. She's never gone *out* to dinner before.

Dad turns off the burners. Trip and I grab our hoodies. Maddie just sort of stands there. She's so happy, she's trembling.

"Do I really get to go, too?" she asks.

"Yes, Maddie," says Mom. I can hear the lump in her throat. It's probably the same size as the one in mine. "From now on, honey, you can go anywhere and everywhere with us."

"Is it chilly out?" asks Maddie.

"Indeed," says E. "The temperature has dropped into the forties, with a twenty-three percent probability of precipitation."

"But I don't even own a jacket," says Maddie. "I never needed one."

"You can borrow mine," I say, handing her my hoodie. "I'll grab my Notre Dame windbreaker."

Maddie pulls my hoodie on over her head. Yes, it's two sizes too big, but it'll keep her warm and toasty.

"Come on, E," says Dad. "You're coming with us, too. You always know what to order."

"Well, sir, I have created a list of the most popular items on Pasquale's dinner menu by cross-referencing several different internet restaurant review sites..."

Everybody heads out the door.

Maddie and I bring up the rear.

She tugs on the sleeve of my blue and gold jacket.

"Sammy?"

"Yeah?"

"Thanks."

"No problem," I say. "You can borrow that as long as you need to."

"No, I mean thank you for giving me the best gift any brother's ever given any sister."

She looks at me with those bright blue eyes.

I don't know what to say.

Fortunately, Maddie does. "You'll always be my very best friend, Samuel Hayes-Rodriguez. Forever." She gives me a strong hug. "Come on," she says. "Everybody's waiting."

We hurry out the back door and pile into the idling SUV.

"Seat belts, please," purrs Soovee.

When we're all buckled up, the autonomous automobile backs out of the driveway and whirs up the road.

"Oh, in all the excitement at school," says Mom, "I forgot to tell you guys I heard from one of those big car company executives."

"And?" says Dad.

"He changed his mind. Now he wants to work with me on my self-driving SUV idea."

"That's fantastic!" I say.

"Way to go, Mom!" adds Maddie.

"Thank you," she says. "But I told him I'd rather keep working on Project Soovee by myself."

"Whaaaat?" I say. "You're turning down all that money?"

"That's right. Soovee had a few false starts and made a couple mistakes. But she's a part of this family now." She pats the SUV's dashboard. "And when you're a member of this family, we never, never, *never* give up on you."

"I know," says Maddie, practically bursting with joy. "Just look at me!"

TOMORROW, I WANT TO PLAY SOCCER, GO WATER-SKIING, PET A CAT, HAVE A PICNIC, JUMP IN A LEAF PILE, GO TO A NOTRE DAME FOOTBALL GAME, RIDE A PONY, SWING ON A SWING, CLIMB A TREE, BUY CANDY, PLAY TAG, CHASE BUTTERFLIES, PICK STRAWBERRIES, MEET A POLICEMAN, BUILD A SAND CASTLE.....
SOOUEE

Sticks and stones
may break your bones,
but mean names
last forever!

GET A SNEAK PEEK AT

AVAILABLE NOW!

Stoopid:
The Origin Story

Okay, the first time I met Michael Littlefield was in the second week of preschool. I remember that, even back when we were just four years old, Michael could crack me up like nobody else. What can I say? He always had a way with words.

"Poop!" he said when I showed him the picture of blue squiggles I'd dribbled off the tip of my brush. "Blue poop."

That, of course, made me giggle. So I told him my name. "I'm David!"

"I'm Michael!"

We toddled back to the art-supplies cabinet because I knew there was still some blue paint left in the jar.

Our teacher, Mrs. Rabinowitz—who always had a headache—wasn't really watching us or paying much attention to anybody. Except her favorite kid, Kaya Kennecky, a girl who came to pre-K every morning in matchy-matchy outfits complete with a matching bow in her curly blond hair.

While Michael and I played with the paint, Kaya sat in Mrs. Rabinowitz's lap reading a picture book about a caterpillar who was ridiculously hungry. So Mrs. Rabinowitz didn't see me dribble paint all over Michael's shoes.

"Poop!" he said. "Blue poop!"

Yes, back then, Michael liked to talk about pee and poop and poopypants because, let's be honest here, when you're a kid in preschool, bodily functions are hysterical. Underpants too.

"Booger butt!" Michael blurted and I cracked up.

Still laughing, I put the blue paint jar back on the shelf. And, yes, I forgot to screw the lid back on.

"Want red?" I asked.

He stuck out his left foot. "Red poop!"

I grabbed the jar of red paint. But the lid wouldn't come off. It was kind of stuck to the dried-out paint. It was like trying to twist open an antique tube of toothpaste.

I'd seen my dad, who was still living with us at the time, bang pickle jars on the kitchen counter when he couldn't twist their lids open. So that's what I did. I banged the jar of red paint against the wobbly steel shelf inside the art-supplies cabinet. I banged it so hard, the lid cracked and flew off. Paint sloshed out all over the place. And all that banging knocked the open blue jar off the shelf too.

Every inch of my hands, face, and clothes that wasn't already speckled red was splattered blue. Michael's clothes were a mess too. But his shoes— squiggly blue and splotchy red—looked incredibly cool (to a four-year-old, anyway).

"Awesomesauce!" we both yelled.

Kaya heard us and saw the disaster we'd made. "Mrs. Rabinowitz!" she hollered. "That stupid boy did something stupid!"

Since I was still holding the jar of red paint in my hand, it was pretty obvious who she was calling stupid.

"You're so stupid, David," Kaya cried. "You're just a stupid-head. You're so stupid, stupid, stupid! You're the stupidest boy ever!"

Everybody in the class started laughing and

pointing and chanting "Stoopid," drawing out the *oo* sound. Mrs. Rabinowitz was busy trying to clean up my mess so she didn't have time to remind everybody that name-calling was strictly against the rules.

I, of course, wasn't laughing. What I did with the paint jars might've been dumb, but that didn't automatically make me *stupid*.

Except it kind of did. It made me Stoopid. With a capital *S*.

Well, to everybody except my paint-spattered partner in crime.

"You're not stupid, David," Michael told me. "You're my best friend!"

If David is stupid, then I must be stupider because I like him.

Stoopid:
The Legend Continues

Things didn't get much better when Michael and I moved up to kindergarten.

Okay, they got way worse. I still did some dumb stuff, like calling the graham crackers we had for snack "grand crappers."

I remember the teacher, Ms. Stone, asked me if I could spell my mom's name. I said, "Yes! M-O-M."

Kaya Kennecky was still in our class. "That boy's name is Stoopid," she told Ms. Stone. "A lot of boys are dumb, but he's the stupidest boy in the whole world!"

"We don't use that word in this class, Kaya," said Ms. Stone.

"Well, what do you call stupid people, then? Idiots?"

I did some other dumb stuff that didn't help my kindergarten reputation any. Once, when I needed Ms. Stone's help tying my shoe, she asked me, "What's the magic word?" I said, "Abracadabra."

When she asked me to try again, I said, "Shazam?"

But does that make me Stoopid or just, you know, a normal kid?

Actually, for a little while, I thought my teacher, Ms. Stone, might be sort of stupid herself. She kept asking us to name all the colors in the crayon box. Didn't she know what they were called? The names were printed right on the wrappers.

In kindergarten, I also had a lot of what they called "excess energy."

You know how some kids act at a birthday party after they eat ice cream and cake and chug soda to wash down all the jelly beans and Laffy Taffy in the goodie bags? That was me on a normal day. I just don't like sitting still, and, unfortunately, a lot of school involves sitting and not fidgeting.

I remember this time when Ms. Stone wanted us to sit on the alphabet rug on the letters of our first names.

I started on the *D*, got bored, scooted over to the *A*, then rolled over to the *V*. Ms. Stone told me she'd meant "just the first letter of your first name."

"Then he should sit on the *S*," said guess who. "For Stoopid!"

She got sent to the corner for that one, which only made her more determined to call me Stoopid every chance she got—just not in front of Ms. Stone.

I don't know why Kaya hated me so much even back then, but I've got to hand it to her: she tried super hard to convince all the other kids to call me that, and it worked. After kindergarten, the name just sort of stuck.